"I don't want to go to church,"

she said. "If I go to church and start my ordinary life all over again, I might as well go home. All my life I've gone to church, been well-behaved, done what I was supposed to do. I'm so used to doing what other people want that I don't even know what I want or who I really am. I'm not a real person. I'm just whatever I'm supposed to be, just dull old reliable M—" She stopped, closing her lips on the name.

He said nothing.

She sighed. "I want something else, something more."

"What do you want?"

"I don't know," she admitted in a very small voice. "I don't know. I asked God to help me know, but He didn't."

"When did you ask?"

"Yesterday," she said and then smiled ruefully. "That isn't much time to wait for His answer, is it? I guess I'd better wait a little longer. Only, what if I never find out? What if He answers and I don't understand the answer? What if I don't even hear it?"

"Are you listening?" asked Adam. "Are you opening your heart to Him and really listening?"

"I don't know," she answered. "Things keep getting in the way. I keep getting involved with people and losing my focus. First there's Bree and the way she is afraid to settle down. Then there's Charlie."

He answered carefully, "I thought that was over."

JANET GORTSEMA lives in Pleasantville, New York, wtih her husband, Frank, and teaches English at Sleepy Hollow High School. *Mockingbird's Song* is her second **Heartsong Presents** novel.

Books by Janet Gortsema

HEARTSONG PRESENTS
HP45—Design for Love

Mockingbird's Song

Janet Gortsema

Heartsong Presents

For Martha,
and for all us other Marthas,
whatever our names

A note from the Author:
I love to hear from my readers! You may write to me at
the following address:· **Janet Gortsema**
Author Relations
P.O. Box 719
Uhrichsville, OH 44683

ISBN 1-55748-770-7

MOCKINGBIRD'S SONG

Cover illustration by Gary Maria.

PRINTED IN THE U.S.A.

one

On February 23, Ewald Phipps proposed to Martha Hollins. This surprised Martha greatly because February 23 was a Friday and Ewald always proposed on Saturday—*every* Saturday. Perhaps he'd thought a Friday proposal would surprise her into acceptance, but Friday or not, Martha's answer was just the same as always: "No."

What, he wanted to know, was she waiting for? He was doing well as an accountant, they had known each other all their lives, and they were expected, by all who knew them, to marry. He had waited long enough—through high school and college, through her beginning years of teaching biology here in Empton, Indiana, and through his beginning years at the office. Now he was 29 and she, 27, and he was ready to set up his own household.

And Martha? She didn't know why she didn't say yes. She just couldn't. Ewald was a nice man, a good man. He was organized, intelligent, kind. She had known him all her life. Wasn't that enough?

Home again that night, in the small upstairs bedroom she had always had, she asked herself that question. She looked her mirrored self straight in the eye and asked—out loud, of course (she did occasionally speak out loud to herself)—if that wasn't enough. Her mirrored self had no answer. Martha studied the reflection intently, trying to find the flaw that made her behave so perversely.

The girl she saw was nice enough looking, tall and straight

and trim, with green eyes that could reduce a class of high school biology students to quiet. She peered at her soft peach skin, accepting the few light freckles and feeling pleasure at its smoothness. It was, she thought, her one good feature. Of course, her hair was a problem. It wasn't red and it wasn't brown, but something in between, and it went where it wanted to go in a mass of untamable curls, kept short in self-defense. She looked reasonably good, she guessed, reasonably normal.

She was steady and dependable, a daughter who remembered her mother's medicine, a sister who was always available for babysitting, a teacher who worried overtime about her students, a church member who attended every Sunday. She loved books and quiet, always had, just as she had always tried to keep peace, to be reasonable, to do what she was expected to do.

Now she was expected to marry Ewald.

"You're a lucky girl to have Ewald," said her mother.

"Ewald will make a fine husband," said her father.

"How many other chances do you think you will have?" said her sister.

So she guessed she should just go ahead and marry him and be done with it.

But. . . .

Did she love him? She supposed she must, but it wasn't like the love she had always dreamed of.. She didn't count the days, much less the hours or minutes, until they met again. His touch did not make her tingle. Worse, neither did his kiss—singular, one each date. Did he tingle at her touch? Good question. If he did, he had never mentioned it.

Was she to go from childhood to marriage without even

a brief period of excitement and/or romance? Evidently. She sighed, twice—once for what was and once for what was not to be.

That was Friday. On Monday she noticed the flyer announcing a one-time special summer program for biology teachers, a work/study program, sponsored by the National Park Service, at the National Seashore installation on Cape Cod. A few "carefully selected teachers" would work on-site for this one summer, "with a view toward sharing their experiences with their colleagues and students on their return to the classroom." *Imagine*, she thought, *a whole summer on Cape Cod. How lovely for some fortunate teachers*. Not her, of course, since she always spent her summers helping her sister with the children and her parents with the house and garden. She was very busy. She couldn't possibly find time to go. Besides, she would never be selected.

On Tuesday, in a wild gesture, she mailed her application. Then, having done that much, she erased it from her mind. It was fun applying, pretending she could go, but she was too practical to hope for more.

In early May, to her total astonishment, she received official notice of her acceptance. She was going, really going. *Alone*. She hadn't thought of that before. She had never gone anywhere alone, not even to college. She had commuted to college from home.

"What will Ewald say?" asked her mother.

"Are you sure you know what you're doing?" asked her father.

"How can you do this to me when you know how much I depend on you?" cried her sister.

"I guess I won't go," Martha said, until Ewald told her

she must go, so she would have her taste of the world and be ready (he hoped) to settle down. He expected her to go. So in early June she went. She loaded her possessions into her blue Chevy sedan, kissed them all good-bye, and drove off for Massachusetts.

It was quiet in the car, even with the radio for company. She wished she had someone along to talk to, to eat with, to read the map. Her mother had insisted she stay overnight with a cousin in Pennsylvania, and she was glad she did. Other than that, she was alone. She drove and thought and thought and drove.

What was she doing alone out here where no one knew her? Having an adventure, that's what. Serious, cautious, old Martha was having an adventure. Old? Twenty-seven is not so old. It just sounds old if your name is Martha. She had always disliked the name. When she had been small she had asked her mother, "How could you name me 'Martha'?"

"You know," her mother had answered. "You're named after my favorite sister and after Lazarus' sister."

"Martha? The sister who was too busy to have time to sit and listen to Jesus? The one who was doing all the work while her sister sat and enjoyed the company?" Martha had groaned.

"I wanted you to have a Bible name," her mother had said.

But Mother, she thought now, *a Martha would not have green eyes and soft peach skin like mine, would not be a slender 5'8" tall, would not have the embarrassing habit of talking to herself. A Martha would look like. . .like Martha Washington*. Martha's russet curls bounced in indignation as she resisted, again, the idea that anybody could see her as a Martha. She wished she were someone else, someone different, someone fun and carefree, maybe a little fluffy. Not *very* fluffy, but a little, instead of reliable and practical and dull.

"I don't want you to be somebody else. I like you the way you are," her mother would have said.

"I don't," said Martha to the car. "I'm nobody going nowhere. I need to be out there with the rest of the world, doing things, having fun. Living."

"You are living," her mother would have said.

"Mother," she said to the car, "I'm 27 years old and still doing the same things I've been doing all my life. My friends have all moved on with their lives and I'm standing still. I need to change. I need to learn a new way to be. I can be anybody I want to be for one whole summer. The National Park Service will never know the difference."

"You'll know," said the mother in her imagination.

"I hope so," Martha said to the car.

That's it, she thought. This one time she wanted to forget what she had been and who she was and reach for what she wanted. And what was it she wanted? She wasn't sure. But she knew it wasn't what she had and what she was. Martha didn't dream of fur coats and trips to Paris. Her wishes were more modest and more difficult to achieve. She wanted to be young and in love and. . .different. She wanted to have a good time, just for one summer, before her life snapped shut.

What she needed, she decided, was a disguise, so she could be someone else for a while—not forever, of course, just for a while. But then she decided it wouldn't work. Too complicated, too melodramatic. Maybe she could just pretend she was someone else. Or maybe she could just call herself another name, a name that fit the person she thought she'd like to be. If she had a different name, maybe she'd feel different—or maybe other people would see her as different. It had possibilities.

All day she played with other names, and by nightfall she had found one to wear for the summer: Muffie. It sounded light (fluffy?), frivolous, fun, new. It sounded just right. By the end of the two long days on the road to Cape Cod she had made up her mind to change, just for the summer. She would be a Muffie.

What a Muffie would do, she would do. *What would a Muffie do?* For one thing, a Muffie would like the new popular music. She could start there. She practiced with the radio, experimentally trying to tune her ears to what was (to her) abrasive music on the car radio. She was not successful. *I'll get used to it*, she thought. *I've spent my life in quiet too long.*

She'd get used to the efficiency apartment in Wellfleet, too. The apartment found and reserved for her by the summer program administrators was scarcely more than a room added by remodeling the upstairs of an old gray shingle house. At first glance it was depressing—hot, stuffy, drab—but she made up her mind she would learn to like it. It would be fun, kind of like camping. Closets were not really necessary, not really. Neither was a full-sized refrigerator. And the tiny stove (stovelet?) would be plenty big. A wall or two would have been helpful, though, to separate the kitchen from the rest of the big room that was living room and bedroom all in one. Ah well, there were three windows and a private entrance at the top of those outside stairs. If the stairs shook like a rope ladder, that was all part of the fun. Best of all, it was undeniably different.

The apartment came complete with a roommate—a tiny, perfect, blond with delicate bones and beautiful blue eyes and enough clothing to outfit Martha's entire fifth period class. Bree, her name was, short for Brianna, and she was in her third summer of lifeguard duty at the Seashore beach.

Perfect, thought the new Muffie. *Bree is just perfect. She's everything I want to be and if I watch her, I can learn to be just like her, except for the smooth curtain of silky blond hair and those tiny bones, of course. I can't copy those. But I can dress as she dresses, think as she thinks, and do as she does.*

"Bree's a great name," said Muffie.

"Muffie's good too," said Bree. "What's it short for?"

"Summer," said Muffie, and laughed. "It's my name for this summer. I want to have a good time here."

"We can do that," said Bree. "Good times are my specialty. We just have to get you acquainted with the gang and you'll be on your way. I have just the man for you to meet." With that, Bree began what turned out to be an entire summer of conversation, chatting of men and clothes and men and parties, and men and the beach, and men.

For lack of closets, she and Bree were forced to find other places for their things. Muffie put up a clothesline above the end of her bed and stacked grocery boxes on their sides, open ends out, under the window. Most of her few things were stowed neatly away in these places.

She did the same for Bree, but that clothesline was full and so were Bree's grocery boxes, and the overflow still covered the tattered sofa, both chairs, part of the little table, and various sections of the floor. Bree seemed to have an inexhaustible supply of clothing and zero interest in taking care of it.

Bree took care of paying the rent to "Old Briggs," since she seemed to know him from another year. It took the whole whirlwind weekend to get settled, begin to get used to each other, buy groceries, make plans, and locate Jack, Bree's romantic interest from last summer. By Monday Bree was on duty and Muffie was ready for orientation. In a few days she was at work in the Salt Pond Visitors' Center, and by Saturday she was ready for her first group presentation on the great storms here along the coast.

Standing just inside the shelter at Marconi Station, waiting for her first "class," she felt the flutter of nervous excitement she always felt on the first day of school. "Ready," she said to no one, and quickly looked around. *I'll have to watch that talking to myself or they'll think I'm crazy,* she thought, fixing her Smokey-the-Bear hat firmly on her head against the brisk sea wind and taking her position in front of the scale model of Marconi's transmitting tower.

She stood quietly, watching the group gather. The family of five on the lookout platform moved toward her, directed there by the Protection Ranger now disappearing over the dune on his rounds. Two older ladies strolled slowly up the walkway in almost matching culottes, straw hats, and walking shoes. The two ladies smiled as they entered the shade of the shelter and settled themselves on the bench attached to the low wall. The family tumbled in and found perches on the top of the low wall in the "window" between wall and roof.

Muffie checked her watch and pulled the map of shipwrecks from her backpack. She'd wait a few more minutes for the young couple down the walk and then begin. As they arrived, she directed them to another perch on the wall.

Muffie cleared her throat and began, "Good afternoon and welcome to Cape Cod National Seashore. I'm Ranger Muffie Hollins, and I'm an interpretive ranger. I'm going to tell you about shipwrecks here on the coast of Cape Cod, but before I do, let's get to know a little bit about each other. I'm from Indiana. Is anyone else here from Indiana? No? Tell us where you're from. How about you?"

Muffie indicated the ladies on the bench, who smiled and responded. *Each one*, Muffie reminded herself; *remember to ask each one*. Drawing on her teaching experience, she worked to establish a friendly atmosphere before going on.

Her small group were warming to each other and to her. When each person had spoken, she spread out her map and held it up so they could see it.

She took a deep breath and began, "Here is a map of the known shipwrecks in this area. You can see that there are many of them all along the coast from the tip of Cape Race on the north to the southernmost point of the cape, the elbow. A famous writer, Henry David Thoreau, once described Cape Cod in this way. . ."

They were paying attention, sitting quietly, expectantly, in front of her, waiting to learn. *It works just like school*, she thought with satisfaction, and went on.

Intent on getting it right, she heard the footsteps but was unwilling to interrupt the flow of her narrative. She merely nodded acknowledgement in the direction of the three latecomers. At a pause, she looked up with a welcoming smile. It was Bree and Jack and—who was this tall, tan, dazzling mass of muscles?

Muffie faltered. The three stepped quietly into the shelter and took places against the wall. The handsome stranger nodded slightly, encouragingly. She found herself gaping foolishly, or at least that's the way she felt, and struggled to break eye contact, to look away from his soft brown eyes.

Where was she? She tried to collect her thoughts. Oh yes. . .up to the part about the waves, her favorite part. She took a deep breath.

"We're going to make some waves," she said to the little group. She stepped to the edge of the shelter and scooped up a double handful of sand. "Now, I'm going to give each of you some sand, so I want you to help me by holding your hands cupped together like this."

She scooped sand from the dune outside the shelter and allowed a small stream of sand to flow through her hands into the waiting hands of the smallest boy, then of the second boy, and so on. Jack and Bree obediently accepted sand. The mass of muscles held out his enormous tanned hands too, and Muffie poured sand into them. She glanced up as she stopped the flow of sand, hands poised above his.

He was grinning.

She looked away quickly. He was laughing at her! She felt a rush of embarrassment warm her face. Her hands trembled, losing some of their sand in a sudden lurch.

She glared at him.

He laughed, showing perfect white teeth.

What nerve he had!

She set her jaw. *He is* not *going to make me lose control on my very first lecture,* she thought. *First I'll do this and do it right. Then I'll deal with him.* She faced the smallest boy. "Now," she said, "hold your hands like this and rub them together. Harder."

She got through it, somehow, demonstrating the abrasive action of wave-driven sand on the bottoms of the ships. She covered the importance of the Nauset Lighthouse and the Lifesavers with their breeches-buoy and their motto, "You have to go out but you don't have to come back." She showed the photos of the tanker *Emmaday,* stranded on the beach one winter, and the photos of damage done by a nor'easter.

She covered it all and, with a relieved sigh, asked if there were any questions. There were a few, including "How do you get to be a Lifesaver?" and "If I find a sunken treasure, can I keep it?" She knew the answers and felt the group was satisfied with her presentation.

"Good-bye and thank you," they said, and left at various speeds down the path, leaving her with Bree, Jack, and the grinning mass of muscles.

Now for him, she thought grimly, and turned with hands on hips.

"You were great," Muscles said before she could speak. "Really great!"

"This is Charlie Cooper," said Bree, beaming like she was offering a gift. "He rooms at Jack's house. He's in P.E.—Physical Education. Charlie, this is Muffie. Shake hands nicely and don't crush her hand before you even get to know her."

"Does that mean he'll crush it later?" asked Muffie, hands behind her back.

He laughed, obediently holding out his hand in greeting. "I never crunch up feisty little redheads. Too dangerous."

Muffie smiled in spite of herself at the thought of anyone thinking of her as either feisty or dangerous, and held out her hand to be enveloped in his massive paw and kept there. She looked up in protest. He smiled down at her with a slow, confident smile that made her uneasy. He gave her hand a little squeeze, then slightly relaxed his hold, allowing her to pull free.

"Most people call me Coach," he said. "You can, if you want to."

Muffie didn't answer. With difficulty she drew her eyes away from that mocking smile and shifted her 124 pounds away from him to stand slightly behind Bree.

"We came to hear your first lecture," said Jack. "It was Bree's idea. She thought it would be fun. Hope we didn't make you nervous."

"Of course not," Muffie murmured.

"You did fine," Bree said, "but of course you would, being a teacher and all. Want to go to P'town with us to celebrate your success? You've never been there and it will be fun."

"Go where?"

"P'town. . .Provincetown. We thought we'd look around a little, catch a bite to eat, show you the town. What do you say?" Clearly Bree had already decided; the question was a formality.

"My car. . . ," began Muffie.

Bree said, "You can't run around P'town dressed like Smokey the Bear. You can make a fast change at the apartment and leave your car there. Jack's driving. Come on." Bree grabbed Jack's arm and started down the path toward the parking lot, her enthusiastic hopping little step making her long, silky blond hair bounce and shimmer in the sunlight. Muffie hesitated. This Charlie and his big white teeth intimidated her. She was not at all sure she was safe with him. *On the other hand,* she thought, *if I wanted to be safe, I should have stayed in Indiana. I said I wanted a new life and here it is staring me right in the face. I got what I wanted and now I'm afraid to take it. What's the matter with me?*

Charlie was dangling her heavy backpack lightly from three fingers. "Ready?" he asked.

"Ready," she answered, and hoped she was.

She gritted her teeth when he draped one heavy arm possessively over her shoulders and swept her at half-lope after the others. In the parking lot she watched the three climb into Jack's roofless, sideless white 4-wheel-drive and roar away in a sandstorm of their own making.

Her ordinary blue Chevy looked sedate and tired compared to Jack's white dust thrower. Rebelliously, she jerked the Chevy into reverse and jammed her foot down on the accelerator. The engine shuddered and stopped.

Flooded, she thought. *Serves me right. Poor old car just isn't made for the fast lane. It's good enough to go back and forth to school until it wears out, but it's not much in a place like this. If I'm not careful, I'll be like that—just good enough to go back and forth to school until I wear out.*

"Not me," she said to the car. "Not if I can help it."

The Chevy's progress to the apartment was maddeningly slow. They were waiting for her out front when she got there. She rushed upstairs and reached for her new lavender shirtwaist dress, the one she had made especially for this summer. On second thought she opted instead for clothes as much like Bree's as she could manage. She exchanged her gray uniform shirt and grayed-green pants for a soft spring-green blouse and white soft pants. She took a quick pass at her face with the washcloth and tried to brush smooth her tangled copper curls. It would have to do.

She dashed down the stairs only a little out of breath and climbed into the back seat of Jack's car as Charlie held the door open. (*Do I call this a car,* she wondered?) She expected Charlie to shut the door and let himself in on the other side, but he slid in after her, so she moved to the far corner to make space between them. He moved over too, filling all the space she had made and then some. There was a lot of Charlie.

He was overpowering, breathtaking. She tried not to look at him, but sat quietly, listening to his voice as he joked easily across the front seat barrier.

"Want to stop at the dunes and let Red here try the big time sand pile?" he was saying.

"Muffie," she said firmly. "My name is Muffie."

"I told you she was feisty," he said to the front seat. To her he said, "Okay, I'll call you Muffie. You call me Coach. Deal?"

"Coach?"

"Not good?" he asked.

"I'd feel like one of your students," she said.

"Okay then, call me Charlie. Deal?"

"Okay. . .Charlie."

He grinned and went back to his conversation with the front seat, allowing her an undisturbed opportunity for a better look at him. In profile he was too handsome to be real, a magnificently carved animal with great strong white teeth flashing against a rich tan. The sun had apparently bleached his hair from a light brown, which was still visible where the wind blew the top layer of pale yellow hair every which way to expose the original color underneath.

The hairs on his massive arms were bleached too, as though he had absorbed the sun, become part of it.

Though tousled by the wind, he had that flawless, carelessly perfect polish of the wealthy. No T-shirt for him. He wore one of those short-sleeved, safari-type shirts she had so far seen only in magazines, and plaid cotton trousers that virtually shouted for notice. Nobody she had ever known had dared wear such trousers. To do so was to invite laughter. She knew, instinctively, that Charlie would enjoy the laughter, would join in and make it his own.

How wonderful, she thought, *to be so confident, so free to do as he chooses.*

He turned at that moment and saw her smiling and smiled back, a genuine smile of open friendliness. She saw that beneath sun-bleached brows his eyes were a warm brown and that they still danced with mischief. This time she found their laughter appealing and laughed back.

"That's better," he said, and stretched his enormous arm across the back of her seat. "You and I will have a good time together. We'll make a great team. Stick with Ol' Charlie and you won't be disappointed."

But will he be disappointed in me? she wondered silently. This was no Ewald Phipps, satisfied with holding her hand on the way home from church. This Charlie was strong, dynamic, demanding. She knew she could handle Ewald, but Charlie was another animal altogether.

Her heart lurched. *Fear? Excitement,* she told herself firmly. This is what she had come here for. All she had to do now was follow Bree's lead and she'd be all right.

In the front seat Jack rested one hand on Bree's shoulder, idly brushing her cheek while he drove. Now and then he turned to look at her, and she gazed into his eyes and crinkled her adorable little nose at him.

I wonder if that would work for me, thought Muffie, giving an experimental crinkle to her classic nose. *No use. Bouncy cheerleader types like Bree can get by with that cute stuff, but I'd feel silly instead of adorable. I'd better stick with normal.*

Normal can't be so bad, she reflected, thinking of the men in Indiana who had said she was attractive. According to them, green eyes and reddish-brown curls were a pretty combination. But then, they were tame men looking for a tame life with a tame girl. *All I know how to be is tame. I'm not exciting enough for this dangerous man with his air of knowing confidence. My one advantage is that he doesn't know how really dull I am. He probably thinks that if Bree and I are friends, we must be very much alike.*

Wrong. But I can watch her and learn. I can fake it. I can act sophisticated like one of those women selling perfume on television, and if I don't make a fool of myself, I just might convince him that I'm a little dangerous myself.

Relax, she told herself, and tried to relax. *Now smile when he looks at you, but only slightly. Let him think you're deciding whether or not he's interesting enough for you. Good. Now look away. Don't look back. Relax.*

This is foolish.

Of course it's foolish. That's what vacations are— chances to look foolish without having your friends watch.

Muffie giggled nervously to herself, then heard her own soft giggle and looked back quickly to see if he had heard.

He was watching. She smiled, carefully, slightly. His interest showed in his eyes and he leaned toward her, abandoning his conversation with the driver.

Her heart lurched again. *Watch it,* she cautioned herself. *Don't overdo it. This man is a handful.*

Charlie pointed ahead on the right where huge bare dunes rose close to the highway. As they came nearer, Muffie could see that while part of these dunes was closed off by snow fence, a large section was accessible to the public.

"Here's your sand pile, Fluffy," Charlie said.

"Muffie," she corrected.

"Right."

Jack explained, "This is one of the few places where the dunes are actually supposed to be climbed on. Dunes look permanent, but they are actually very fragile. Any traffic at all on the dunes, even an occasional barefooted walker, breaks down the thin protective layer of vegetation that holds the sand in place. When that happens, the dunes disintegrate. They move or blow away with the winds or collapse into the sea.

"This little section of dunes is open to satisfy everybody's natural desire to climb on a dune and see for himself what it's like. I suppose the conservationists hope that people will stay off the other dunes if they sacrifice this one.

"You can tell I teach earth science," Jack laughed, slowing the car to a stop in the parking area at the foot of the dune.

Before the car was fully stopped, Charlie had jumped out. He ran around to Muffie's side of the car.

"Pick up your feet," he ordered, grasping Muffie's waist with two huge hands as she rose to get out of the car. With no visible effort at all, except for the muscles shifting under the tan skin of his massive arms, he lifted her out of the car and set her on the sand.

"About 120 pounds, I'd guess," he said, his hands still on her waist.

She grasped his wrists to pull his hands away. It was like grasping stone. He smiled down at her.

"Am I close?" he asked, not moving.

"Close," she answered, thinking, *too close*. Then he released her and began to climb, leaving her to struggle in his wake through the deep sand.

It was difficult going. Her feet sank so far in with each step that she had to take giant climbing steps to get anywhere at all. At ten feet up, she pulled off her sandals rather than ruin them. At twenty feet she leaned forward to scramble up on all fours, shoe straps clutched in one hand. At forty feet she was hot, out of breath. She looked up to see Charlie grinning down at her from another twenty feet above her head.

"Need help?" he asked.

"No," she said, standing still, ankle deep in sand.

His grin widened. He slid down almost to her and reached out one hand to help her. She took it and felt herself lifted until her feet skimmed lightly over the heavy sand, climbing easily to the windy crest.

"Thanks," she said as she straightened to look around. "I guess I'm a little out of shape."

"Don't worry; I'll have you toughened up in no time. They don't call me Coach for nothing."

She shut her eyes against the thought of toughening up, especially if it involved more climbs. *How did Bree manage to climb this?* She looked behind her to discover that Bree and Jack were still in the car, vehicle, whatever. "They didn't climb," she said inanely.

Charlie shrugged, "They've seen it before. When you've

seen one dune, you've seen 'em all. Race you down?"

"I just got here," she objected, "and I'm probably never coming back." On the other side of the dune lay more sand and then the Atlantic Ocean, stretching forever into the horizon and past it. "Ohhhh," she breathed, captured by the majesty of the sea.

"Nice view," offered Charlie. "Ready to go?"

Muffie sighed and reluctantly turned away to begin the slip-slide descent. Reaching up to her this time, Charlie held out a steadying hand, which she grasped without hesitation. Going down was easier than going up, but it still took effort.

"Thanks," she said again at the bottom. "I can manage from here."

He seemed not to hear. He did not let go of her hand until they reached the car. She was afraid he was going to lift her in, but he only opened the door to allow her to clamber in and then he slid in after her. It seemed reasonable for him to assume his usual two-thirds of the seat.

"P'town?" asked Jack.

"Right," answered Charlie and Bree in what must have sounded like a unanimous vote to Jack, who promptly revved up the engine and roared out of the sand and onto the highway.

With the jerk into action, Muffie's head snapped backward and then snapped forward at the first gear change. She struggled to regain her poise. No one noticed. *That's a blessing,* she thought. *Or was it?*

Blessing. She hadn't heard that word around here, and she wasn't likely to hear it unless she was the one who said it. Losing that word from her vocabulary would take a little work. She had grown up with it, had been taught to say a blessing before each meal, had been told to "Count your blessings," had heard over and over the expression, "It's a blessing that. . ." According to her mother, there were blessings everywhere.

"Amen to that," her father would have said.

Well, maybe they were right about their lives being full of blessings, but to Muffie the same life was just stifling. As she had grown to feel more and more closed in by it, she had lost interest in the details of that life. She no longer cared about the height of the corn by the 4th of July nor about the date of the first hard frost. She wanted out, if only for one free summer. If "out" meant a summer without blessings, that was fine with her.

Wasn't it?

When she had second thoughts like this she wondered if she really did know what she was doing. She must stop this.

"No second thoughts," she said.

"What did you say?" said Charlie.

"No. . ." Muffie unfuzzied her thoughts and returned to reality to find Charlie leaning toward her attentively.

"No what?" he prodded.

"Um. . .no. . .um. . .no cloud in the sky today," she invented.

He looked up. "Nope. Perfect day for the beach."

Bree swung her head around. "You and your beach. Is that all you think of?"

"Nope," said Charlie, studying Muffie's face intently until she looked away in confusion.

"Don't turn away," he said. "I like that funny face of yours. I was just counting your freckles." He reached out to touch her gently on the cheek.

She sat very still, not looking at him, not looking any place.

"You don't like that, do you," he said, and it was not a question.

"I don't know you well enough to like it," she answered.

His finger traced the side of her cheek. "You will," he said. "I promise." He tapped her lightly on the nose and chuckled. Then he slowly sat back in his own two-thirds of the seat.

Muffie released a long slow breath, as quietly as she could. *He scares me*, she thought. *Why? Because he does things and says things I'm not used to? So does Bree, but she doesn't scare me. Because he's so big? Maybe that's it. That must be it. It's this feeling that he could crush me with one hand if he wanted to. That and the fact that I don't know whether he might just want to.*

Don't be silly, she scolded herself. *If Bree thought he was dangerous, she wouldn't have brought him along for me.*

Relax.

Smile. . .slightly, mysteriously.

two

The mysterious smile was stiff on Muffie's lips by the time they reached the center of Provincetown. The powerful white car chortled to slow motion on tight old streets lined with houses from at least a hundred years ago. They slowed for approach and came to a standstill at the choked intersection of the old whaling village's primary shopping street, appropriately named Commercial Street, and the wider street to the municipal pier.

People thronged the intersection, the sidewalks, and the middle of the shopping street itself as far right or left as Muffie could see.

"What's happening?" she asked, looking for fire trucks or parade barriers.

"Saturday night in P'town," said Jack. "This is where it all happens."

"Where what happens?"

"Anything. Everything. It's a good-time town—part Disney, part New England, part pure craziness. I'll drive down Commercial and you can see for yourself." Jack eased the car carefully through a right turn onto the shopping street and she looked.

Ice cream stands and souvenir shops competed with T-shirt displays and craft shops. Pedestrians and bicyclists twined and intertwined their paths, now and then very casually moving aside to make barely enough space for a car or two to creep through. A blasé teenage boy coasted by on skates, grazing the curb on one swerve, nudging a car on another, all without change of expression. Although the car crept through the crowd only slightly faster than someone walking, she couldn't look fast enough to see it all.

"Is it always like this?" she asked.

"Only in summer," answered Jack. "The Cape is a different place in winter. Then we locals take over again, and the town belongs to the fishing fleet and the artists and the other full-time residents. I think I prefer the winter, really."

"But there's nothing to do here in the winter," objected Bree. "I don't know how you get along."

"Just like everyone else in the world does, I guess," said Jack. "We store up enough fun in the summer to last us through the cold."

"Not me," said Bree. "I like action and people and good times. Don't you, Muffie?"

"Definitely." Muffie sounded determined, even to her own ears, thinking that she, too, had to store up enough good times for the cold, maybe even enough for the rest of her life.

"I like the way you girls think," agreed Charlie. "Let's grab up the good times."

At the end of the most crowded section, Jack turned right again to get to a faster street two blocks over. After a few blocks he drove into a parking lot. "The only way to see the town is to walk," he announced. "Everybody out."

Crossing the street, they descended a few stairs and cut through a side walkway almost too small to be a street, although it boasted a street sign. On both sides were two- and three-story houses that looked quite old. Many were remodeled into vacation apartments, studios, and rooming houses, with modern skylights and decks stuck here and there in old walls and roofs. At the end of the short "street," they found themselves in the midst of the strolling crowd on Commercial Street.

For the most part the strollers moved along with easy, relaxed grace. With no sense of urgency, no hint of intent to arrive at a particular place at a particular time, people seemed to walk and look for the mere pleasure of seeing and being seen.

Along the sides, on curbs, benches, railings, and porches, people rested and watched the passersby. Some sat in open windows above the narrow street. Dogs trotted back and forth in loose proximity to owners. A monkey peered down at Muffie from his perch atop a passing shoulder. Babies slept in backpacks while their parents enjoyed the evening. Old people and young moved side by side, forward and across and back. The human tide moved and milled in the amiable ease of a crowd in relaxed pursuit of pleasure.

"Belgian waffles," read Charlie. "Sounds good to me."

"All food sounds good to you, Charlie," laughed Bree, crinkling her nose at him.

"True, true," Charlie said, passing the Belgian waffles by. "This is Muffie's first taste of P'town, so we ought to eat whatever she wants. What'll it be, Muffie?"

She answered immediately, "Anything. Anything at all, just so it's real food and something I've never tasted before."

Bree skipped a couple of steps in excitement. She said, "If you mean that, I've got the very place for you— the little place on the corner next to the sandal maker. You know the place I mean, Jack?"

"The raw bar?" he asked.

"Right," said Bree. "The very thing."

"I don't know about that," Jack said.

Bree said, "Sure. She'll love it. Won't she, Charlie?"

Aware of a glint of mischief in Bree's blue eyes, Muffie asked, "A bar?"

"No," said Bree, "a place that serves raw fresh food."

"Fine," said Muffie. "I like salad."

Charlie laughed loudly. "Did you two hear that? She says she likes salad. Let's get her some salad."

"What's funny?" said Muffie.

Charlie only laughed again.

The raw bar was far down the street, and they were in no hurry. Along the way they wandered in and out of whatever shops caught their attention. In one arcade Muffie stood entranced by shelf after shelf of seashells from all over the world, labeled and priced. Bree lingered over silver earrings. Charlie paced up and down the aisles, restless, while Jack found acquaintances among those behind the counters and stopped to pass the time of day.

The fragrant aroma of fresh bread drew them to the Portuguese bakery, but Bree pulled them past it, promising to return if they were still hungry later. She intercepted Charlie's move to the empty table at the sidewalk café, too.

Near the town hall/police headquarters, they heard music and wandered around to the other side of the building to stand with others for part of a folk music concert. At a break in the music, Bree pulled them back to the main street, herding them past the open door of the salt water taffy shop.

"Kites!" shouted Charlie, and he disappeared. The others followed up the steps to a big old house bedecked with windsocks and oriental kites catching the evening breeze from poles in the front yard.

Inside were more kites: plastic ones, and paper, and floating silk. They hung from the ceiling and covered the walls and took up space on the uneven wooden floor, leaving a meandering path among the displayed wares. They found Charlie in the back room, gazing up at five silk triangles attached one above the other.

"Aren't those triangles something?" he demanded.

"They're lovely," agreed Muffie, "but aren't they a little tricky to fly?"

"Of course. That's the fun— much better than a single delta. A delta's so stable it'll fly all day tied to a chair. Boring."

"How about a small dragon?" suggested the salesgirl, who had come up behind them. "That's a rainbow dragon right above your head. They're responsive and frisky without being difficult to manage."

"Sounds like the perfect woman," said Charlie.

He's brash and crude, Muffie thought. Her face showed her objection to Charlie's comment. "Charlie. . ."

He laughed. To the clerk he said, "She's feisty." Then he laughed again at Muffie's glare and pointed to the ceiling.

Muffie looked up to see a long, tapering kite suspended loop after loop across the ceiling. "It's beautiful," she said, "like a silken ribbon. But it's so long. I don't think. . ."

"Of course you can," said Charlie. "We'll take it."

"It's too expensive," she objected.

"We have mylar dragons," said the clerk. "They're much less expensive than nylon and fine for beginners. . ."

"Fine," said Charlie. "The fifty-foot one, and string and

a swivel."

"Twenty-five foot," said Muffie.

"Twenty-five foot mylar and string and a swivel," said the clerk, who knew what the customers should have even if they didn't know.

"Thank you," said Muffie, as Charlie paid.

He said, "Here. It's yours. You carry it. Now let's eat."

The raw bar was just across the main intersection, identified by a homemade sign that was easy to miss. The little wooden shack was not more than an open stand with no seats out front and no door to go inside. There was only a rough counter with holders for paper napkins. Oil drum trash containers flanked the ends of the counter. To Muffie it looked rough and shabby, but customers crowded so thickly around it that she couldn't see past them to the inside.

With help from Jack and Charlie, they worked their way up to the counter where Muffie could see what people were eating. "What are those things in clam shells lying on the crushed ice?" she asked.

"Clams," said Charlie, "raw clams and oysters. That's why they call this a raw bar."

"Where do they cook them?" Muffie asked, looking for and not finding a stove.

"They don't. You eat them raw."

Muffie's stomach lurched. "Raw?"

"Raw and alive. That way you're sure they're fresh. What's the matter?"

Muffie couldn't take her eyes off the clams. "But Charlie, you don't even kill them?"

"You do if you bite into them. Otherwise, I guess your digestive juices kill them. They're supposed to be eaten this way. Come on, Duffy; I'll show you."

"Muffie," she said, backing up a step. "That's okay. A hamburger would be fine."

Bree taunted, "I thought you wanted to try something new."

Muffie felt queasy. "I do, really. It's just that. . .they look so. . .slippery."

"Try one, just one," said Charlie. "I'll order a dozen and you can have one of mine."

The dozen on the counter in their little paper container looked bigger and bigger. Muffie watched Charlie and then Bree and Jack as each picked up a clam, shell and all. She peered in to see if the little mollusks were breathing. She couldn't tell.

Charlie squeezed lemon on his clam and held the shell to his mouth. He tipped it up, swallowed, and put the empty shell on the counter.

"See?" said Charlie, "nothing to it. Here." He held out a shell to Muffie.

Muffie's stomach heaved uncomfortably. Bree laughed and up-ended her shell. She was still laughing as she chewed. Muffie felt a little green.

Jack said, "You don't have to eat one it you don't want to. I don't eat cabbage. Can't stand the stuff."

"Maybe another time," said Muffie.

"Maybe never," said Bree, daring, challenging.

"Nothing to it," said Charlie.

Muffie gulped. *Now or never*, she thought. *If I don't try. . .*

She took the wet, slippery clam from Charlie and pulled it out of its shell, tugging it loose, certain it was hanging on for dear life. In her fingers it was not as slippery as she had expected. *Quick*, she thought, *before I change my mind*. She popped it into her mouth and clapped her hand over her mouth to keep it there.

It sat on her tongue. She blinked, half expecting to feel it move. She tried to swallow, but it wouldn't go down. She could feel her throat start to close.

"Chew," said Bree, so Muffie chewed.

I killed it, she thought, and chewed some more. She was grateful to discover that the clam was muscular and not slippery, and it helped to know that the thing was now dead. A few more desperate chews and then a giant swallow and it was gone. She resisted an almost overwhelming urge to bring it back.

Cheers from Charlie and Jack made her feat official. She smiled shakily, tasting the strange flavor still in her mouth and hoping the clam would stay where it was.

At her elbow Bree said, "Another one, Muffie? Only one left."

"Mine," said Charlie, and swallowed it whole. "Now, let's see about some real food instead of just appetizers. What next, Muffie? Fried crab?"

She hoped not.

"I could go for one of Mario's wedges," volunteered Jack. "How's that?"

"What is it?" asked Muffie, trying not to sound cautious.

"Basic stuff—a fat sandwich. Some places they're called heroes, or submarines, or hoagies. It's okay. Honest."

Jack sounded believable, so Muffie voted for a wedge. A few minutes later she was sitting on a step with a normal-looking ham and cheese wedge in her hand.

"Beer for everybody," announced Charlie, putting four

cans down on the top step.

"No thanks," Muffie said lightly.

"No beer? You don't like clams and now you don't like beer." Charlie shook his head. "What kind of life do you live out there in Indiana?"

"Life there is just like it is here, only different," said Muffie, trying to answer without actually explaining.

"That clears it up," said Jack, and they all laughed. "Now get the lady something she can drink, Charlie. She's earned it. Lemonade?"

Muffie nodded and Charlie obligingly went for lemonade.

"Charlie doesn't understand anybody who can turn down a beer," said Bree.

Jack studied Muffie thoughtfully and said, "I have a feeling there are quite a few things about you he's not going to understand."

Privately agreeing with him, Muffie's only response was a rueful half smile. Adapting to this new lifestyle was more difficult than she had expected. She never knew when one of her cautious old ways would trip her up and betray her. *When in doubt*, she thought, *be quiet*.

Bree said, "If you ask me—"

"Hey, there's the professor! Professor! Over here, Professor," Jack shouted, jumping up and waving his arm.

Bree groaned aloud, "Oh, no!"

An arm waved back above the heads and then a face emerged from the crowd. As the professor came closer and stopped next to the step she sat on, Muffie caught her breath.

He was lean and tall, very tall, so that even though she sat on the top step and he stood on the ground on the other side of the railing, she still had to look almost straight up to see his face.

As Jack introduced them, the professor looked down at her and she saw that his eyes were blue and deep as the sea itself. His mouth smiled politely, but the serious eyes studied her intently.

"Muffie?" The professor was verifying her name.

She nodded vaguely and offered her hand for him to shake.

He looked at the proffered hand, which still held her nibbled-on ham and cheese wedge. "No, thank you," he said politely as he took a closer look at this slender young woman. His glance rested on soft full lips and smooth skin and returned to the startling green eyes. He added, "If you don't mind, I'll join you for a few minutes."

He sauntered easily around the railing and settled his lanky frame on the step below Muffie's feet, resting his back against the railing.

"Are you here for a vacation?" he asked Muffie.

"No. . .yes. . .sort of," she answered.

He waited for further explanation, but Muffie thought of none.

"She's a seasonal, interpretive," explained Bree.

"Interpretive," he repeated, sounding as if he thought it unlikely. She wondered if it was because she hadn't made sense. "Do you teach in the winter?"

"Um—" she responded.

"Yes, she does," said Bree.

"I see," said the professor, sounding as if he didn't see at all.

Charlie returned with lemonade for Muffie, greeted the professor, and sat down to inhale his wedge. Muffie listened as the conversation moved quickly from light chat to serious talk as Jack compared notes with the newcomer on recent sightings of some kind. As the professor became more and more animated in the discussion, his lean face came alive and the blue depths of his eyes sparkled with interest. He talked with his hands, using them to emphasize his words. They gestured with sinuous grace, and she found herself fascinated by their movements.

Everything about him was intense, she decided: his eyes, his black unruly hair, black except for a trace of white at the temples, his straight dark eyebrows, his wide, serious mouth. Everything but his clothes, which were clean but careless, almost shabby. His jeans were worn to threadbare spots at the knees, and his faded sweatshirt sported holes in the elbows to match the holes in his jeans. He dressed as if what he wore was too unimportant to occupy thought or time.

Her eyes returned to his and found them watching her with the same intensity she had felt in his talk. He seemed to be waiting for an answer to some question she had been too preoccupied to hear.

She looked at Bree, who was regarding her with some amusement. Bree spoke for her again, "Not yet. She hasn't had time. She and Charlie are. . ."

"You're with Charlie," the stranger said, blue eyes steady on Muffie's green ones. Muffie nodded. The professor looked Muffie over, assessing, frowning slightly, and she felt sure there was some obscure disappointment in the look, some disapproval behind his scrutiny. "Hmmm," he said, and turned back to his conversation with Jack.

Feeling as if she had been dismissed, Muffie refused to be shut out and began to follow the conversation. As she listened, she learned that the sightings they found so engrossing were sightings of whales. Putting one piece with another she came to the conclusion that "the professor" really was a professor, and that he was involved in some kind of study of whales.

Whatever it was, it totally absorbed him and she found it gradually began to interest her too. She scarcely noticed Charlie's departure and return with another wedge. She forgot her earlier dazed reticence and, urged by her natural curiosity, began to ask questions. Her knowledge of whales was book knowledge, a smattering of information about their biological functions but little about their world. Although her questions were no doubt elementary, the professor answered her with as much respect as he would demonstrate in answering difficult questions from his colleagues. She was unaware that he phrased his answers carefully so that she would feel comfortable in asking more. She knew only that he and his whales were fascinating.

Shuffling and pacing next to her, Charlie was impatient to be done with the conversation. Bree was too. Finally brought to awareness by their blatant signaling, Jack stood, saying with regret, "We have to go."

The professor nodded in understanding and took his leave. He took three long steps away from them and turned back. He spoke to Muffie alone, "If you'd like to see the whales sometime, come out on the boat."

"I'd like that," she said.

Almost as an afterthought, he spoke to the others, "Come anytime. Just let me know." He nodded a general good-bye and strode off, the only person on the street moving with purposeful speed.

Bree said irritably, "Next time we see one of Jack's professors on the street, try to pretend we don't know him. We wasted more than an hour with his boring whales."

"I didn't think they were boring," said Muffie.

"We know," said Bree. "If you had asked one more question I was going to step on your fingers. Let's go. It's almost seven-thirty and we've covered only half of this place."

"Wind's up," said Charlie, lifting his face to the sharp breeze. "I say we fly the new kite a while before we do any more shopping."

Charlie led them to the municipal pier and then off into the sand of the beach behind the shop buildings of Commercial Street. There he fixed the swivel onto the arched face of the dragon and firmly attached the cord to the swivel. He tossed the kite into the air, allowing it a little string for a start, and tugged and coaxed it until it hung like a rainbow in the sky over the beach.

The long, many-colored tail unfurled as the face pulled it skyward. It rippled and stretched, moving like a live thing against the clouds. When Charlie was satisfied that the kite was properly in place, he beckoned Muffie to him. Placing the twine roll in her hand, he stood behind her, reaching around her to demonstrate the method for flying kites.

He was too close. She felt trapped, smothered, confused. He seemed not to notice, but went about the business of placing her hands correctly and explaining when to tug and when not to tug. Gradually, she resigned herself to his closeness and began to pay attention to his instructions.

"Now you've got it," he encouraged, and he let go, stepping back. Relieved and confused all at once, she let out the loop of string she had held in her right hand. Immediately the kite dived. "Pull," he ordered. She did and was amazed to see the kite rise steadily upward again.

"Do that again," he instructed. "Let out some string."

Again the dragon plunged toward earth.

"Tug," he said, and again the dragon rose and steadied.

"I've got it; I've got it!" she cried. Experimentally loosening and tugging, she played the kite into dips and dives and loops and climbs until her arms ached.

For almost an hour she played like a child next to this giant, and he had patiently led her into it. She looked up at him, astonished. This was a side of him she hadn't expected. She had thought he would demand attention for himself all the time, but he'd obviously enjoyed her pleasure in the kite. He was kind—a little crude, but kind. And fun. There was more to this man than just muscle.

She watched him carefully fold the kite as she held the rainbow ribbon taut in the stiff breeze. Bree and Jack appeared from up the beach where they had wandered while the dragon had been in the air.

The four drifted toward the shops of Commercial Street again and wandered up and back, covering every shop that was still open, which was most of the shops. Instead of dispersing, the crowd thickened and became a huge party. Some sang and laughed as they strolled, and Muffie absorbed the mood of it, humming little snatches of tunes to herself now and then.

They sampled and tasted South Seas frappe, which was the most delicious kind of milkshake Muffie had ever tasted—fruit-flavored and luscious; fried whole crabs, which squished in her mouth like enormous spiders; cranberry sherbet to erase the taste of the crab; salt water taffy; and Portuguese deep-fried dough. She tasted it all.

Charlie stopped them for another beer at an outdoor café. Uncomfortable with the drinking, Muffie stuck to lemonade. *Grow up*, she told herself. *You're out in the big world with people who know how to have fun. Mother's not watching and there's no one to tell you not to drink beer if you want to.*

She was less uncomfortable when Jack also ordered lemonade. *I'll get used to it*, she thought, and sipped her lemonade.

"Who's the professor?" she asked during a lull in the conversation.

"My marine bio prof from grad school, Professor Stowe," said Jack. "The best teacher I ever had. He's here for post-doctorate research on cetaceans. Stays here in P'town near the research ship."

"Did he mean what he said about going out with him on the boat to see the whales?" Muffie asked.

Bree said, "Of course. He's always trying to get people to go see his whales. It's almost a mission with him. You ought to go once. You might like it."

"Let's all go," Muffie suggested.

Bree said, "We've all been."

"If you've seen one whale, you've seen them all," said Charlie, making Muffie wince.

Somebody suggested leaving and they drifted toward the car, taking a half hour to get there. The night was chilly with the breeze from the sea, and the car was even chillier as it sped through the night.

There was little banter in the car. Absorbed in each other, Jack and Bree left Charlie and Muffie to their own conversation in the back seat.

As Charlie crowded nearer, taking three-quarters of the seat and moving toward four-fifths, Muffie sought nervously for ways to divert his attention. She spoke of the kite and of Provincetown and of the traffic and of the weather. The weather was a poor choice because Charlie pointed out that she was shivering and that she might get warm if she got closer.

Instead, she searched her brain for something to distract him. "Get a man started on his favorite subject and he'll talk for hours," her father always said. But what was his favorite subject? She tried music. No. Politics. No. Travel. No. Football. Yes! One or two prodding questions got him started and that was all it took. As he warmed to the topic, he forgot that she might be cold. He talked on and on about his old days on the university team, his wins and losses, his hopes for a pro career, his injuries. He was still talking enthusiastically when they pulled up in front of the gray-shingle house in Wellfleet.

"I'm home," she pointed out to him and laughed at his surprise. When he apologized for boring her, she laughed again and said truthfully that she wasn't bored at all. She added, "I can't get out."

"That's the idea," Charlie said.

"Not my idea," she answered, pulling her feet up under her on the seat so she could climb up and over the side of the open car. As she stood, Charlie growled in resignation and ordered her to wait for him. He climbed up and over his own side and came around to lift her out on her side.

"Put me down, Charlie," she ordered, clutching at his hair to steady herself. Instead, he sat her on his shoulder and, with Muffie frightened and wobbling at the height, climbed the stairs to the apartment door, where he demanded the key.

"No key, Charlie. You can't come in. Landlord's orders. Put me down, Charlie. Please." She hoped he would.

He lifted her off his shoulder and held her against the door, her face almost level with his, and leaned toward her for what she knew was about to be a very determined kiss.

"No, Charlie," she said, beginning to panic.

His face came closer. She could not escape the smell of beer.

"NO!" she said loudly, bringing her arm up to push against his throat.

Unexpectedly, he laughed aloud. "Okay, Stuffy, you win, this time," he said, and lowered her slowly until her toes touched the floor before he let her go.

"Muffie," she said.

With another laugh, he patted her on the head like a small child and trotted off to the car, where he vaulted into the back seat and settled down to wait for the other couple to finish saying good night.

She was trembling as she took her key from her pocket and had to steady her hand against the door to ease the key into the lock. At last she got the door open and slipped quickly inside.

That was close, she thought, but she had escaped. This time. *What about next time?* Maybe there wouldn't be a next time. But he was so beautiful, like something from a book.

"Make up your mind, Stuffy," she said in the dark room. "First you want to run on the fast track, and then you don't. If you want to have fun like Bree and see for yourself what real life is like, you'd better get used to more than raw clams."

I can't, she thought.

You can, she told herself, switching on the light in the living-sitting-eating-junk-work room.

What a mess! She surveyed the heaps and piles of clothing, boxes, and other paraphernalia with the same dismay she always felt when she came into the room. Muffie sighed and plucked a yellow sandal from the sofa back, wondering idly where the other sandal was.

From the small front window she could see the white car still parked in front with Charlie stretched out in the back seat and Bree and Jack together in the front seat. Bree might be a mess with her clothes, but she certainly knew how to live. No quiet life for her. No insecurities. No long, empty summer days. Or evenings. Bree knew how to get along.

Bree wouldn't have minded a little kiss from Charlie.

"There must be something wrong with me," said Muffie to the window.

Bree was getting out of the car. Another kiss or two at the door, and she'd be here in the room all happy and bouncy and wide awake, asking questions about Charlie and how Muffie liked him.

"Not tonight," said Muffie. She pitched the yellow sandal into Bree's corner and scrambled to change into pajamas and get into bed before Bree could catch her for a long, late night of interrogation. She dived into the narrow bed and pulled up the covers. Remembering that she had dropped her clothes in disorder, she jumped up to snatch the discarded clothing and stuff it hurriedly into the laundry bag and hop back into bed.

She listened. There was no sound at the door. She stretched and turned toward the wall. When at last Bree came in, Muffie seemed to be sound asleep.

three

A particularly loud bird woke Muffie. Six-thirty, her watch said. She lay listening to the bird's song rise and fall in complicated patterns and trills, all unfamiliar to her.

She concentrated, trying to find the beginning of the song and frame it in her mind to keep, but she found it constantly varied and wondered if he made up his song as he went along. She figured he must be a wonderfully beautiful little bird to sing like that—perhaps one of those little yellow-and-black ones she'd glimpsed a few days ago. After all those biology courses, she knew a lot about cells and amoebas and very little about the birds, fishes, and mammals around her. Some biologist! There was so much more to know.

She quietly rose, selected the top pair of jeans and the top shirt in each pile, and dressed soundlessly. Finished with the quick grooming, she scribbled a note for Bree, snatched an apple with one hand and her sneakers with the other, and slipped like a shadow from the room and down the stairs in the chilly morning.

She stopped to put on her sneakers and take the measure of the morning air, then headed at a steady pace down the road toward the harbor. In the cool morning Charlie seemed never to have happened.

West Main Street, Wellfleet, was almost as quiet as her room. The dozen or so shops were closed and the lively activity of the typical business day was almost entirely absent. Only one car passed her, going the opposite way, and then a battered pickup truck with a golden retriever in back sniffing the air rattled toward the harbor.

She was passing the Lighthouse Restaurant, which apparently had nothing to do with lighthouses, when the Town Hall clock struck six. *Six?* She looked at her watch and then remembered that she had read about the clock, that it was the only land-clock in the world to strike ship's time.

Her watch said seven, so six bells must mean seven o'clock in ship's time. Six bells. She liked that. Even the clock here was different from the one at home.

She passed the corner general store and turned down Commercial Street (another one?), where art galleries in old houses hadn't yet opened for the Sunday tourists. Farther on, Lobster Hutt's (with two t's, which she wondered about) mannequin fisherman pulled his net to the boat fastened to the roof of the popular restaurant. At last, over a little rise, she glimpsed the sea—Wellfleet Harbor on Cape Cod Bay, to be exact.

Small houses on the left and a restaurant on her right failed to catch her interest. She looked to the sea and picked up her pace in her hurry to reach it.

The parking lot at the municipal pier was dotted with the cars of those as eager to be at the sea as she, and a few people already moved about the docks or on moored boats. Out on the pier itself she recognized the pickup truck that had passed her, the dog still in the back.

From the edge of the pier she looked down at the boats below. They weren't the sleek fiberglass sailboats she had expected. They were grubby and worn, with great hooks and pulleys and rusted tangles of metal. Working boats, belonging to the local shellfishermen, she supposed. Surprised that they were working on Sunday, she decided it must be harder to make a living at fishing than she had thought.

She watched men ready their boats, listening to their companionable banter back and forth from boat to boat. Two men or maybe three to a boat, they started noisy engines, dropped their lines, and chugged away toward the bay. There seemed to be no pattern in their going and not all boats left.

Perhaps they had to catch the tide. Muffie knew about tides but, again, only from books. Was the tide up now and going out, or was it still coming in? She couldn't tell. She tried to determine the direction of the waves, but to her they seemed to go up and down, not in any other particular direction. She wished she knew.

With most of the fishing fleet gone, she settled down on the outside edge of the pier, leaning against a piling, and lifted her eyes to the smaller boats bobbing about on tether in the harbor. These were more what she had expected to see—pleasure craft, mostly sailboats with bare masts. In the outer harbor one large sailboat rode toward the bay and several small ones with colorful sails played with the wind.

How lovely, she thought, *to move across the surface of the water without the grinding noise of an engine, to feel the sail catch the wind*. In her mind she sailed with them, trying to know the feeling secondhand. She imagined it must feel almost like being a human kite.

Maybe someday she'd go out there on a small boat with a rainbow sail. Someday she'd know someone who'd say, "Let's go for a sail," and she'd say, "Sure," very casually, as if she did such things every day.

Maybe Bree knows somebody with a boat.

She took a bite of her apple.

She blinked.

"The professor," she said. He had a boat, or at least he used one, and he had invited her to go out on it. Actually he'd invited all of them, but she couldn't help feeling that the invitation had been especially for her—maybe it had been the way he had seemed to speak directly to her, as if the others hadn't been there. No, it had been something in his eyes.

Those deep blue eyes looked back at her from her memory, and she felt again the shock of their gaze. She had looked up to find him next to her and the next few minutes had become a blur of deep blue eyes and dark unruly hair and lean, expressive hands. Even later, when she had been more accustomed to his presence on the step below her and had recovered from the initial daze, she'd felt unusually drawn to him.

Nonsense, she thought. *It must be my imagination. Or the raw clam. That would have made anybody feel strange. Or maybe it was the ambiance of the place and the time.*

Either way, clam or influence of the evening, he had invited her to go out on his boat to see the whales. Last night she'd enjoyed hearing about them and now she found the idea of learning more about them intriguing. If the whales turned out to be boring, she would at least have had a chance to get out in a boat. The more she thought about it, the better it sounded. She just might go.

She looked at her apple with its one bite gone and finished it. She'd go.

She rose, crossed the pier to drop her apple core in the trash container (along with a candy wrapper she found lying on the pavement), and started back to the apartment, stirred by one of those streaks of energy that she got when she made up her mind to do something. As she marched along, she sang under her breath and made plans.

The town clock struck two bells as she crossed the yard to her stairs. Nine o'clock, her watch said. *Ship's time*, she thought, and smiled.

A church bell pealed not far away. It was Sunday and time for church, just as it had been every Sunday morning of her life as far back as she could remember. Except for rare days of illness or accident, she had been in church at least once, usually twice, almost every Sunday. Her family had always gone together, four of them when her sister still lived at home, and then three.

Two of them this morning, she realized, her mother and father side by side, no doubt thinking of her, praying for her.

For the first time since she'd left, she was homesick. She missed them. She wondered who was seeing that her mother took her medicine and who was feeding Whiskers.

Not that she would go back right now—not when things were going so well here. But she would miss going to church. She'd missed it last Sunday, even in the confusion of getting settled here. So why not go to church here? But of course she didn't know anyone here in these churches, wouldn't even know which to go to. She'd probably feel lost in a church full of strangers who'd see her as one of the summer people, one of the outsiders.

What was she thinking of? Something serious and sensible! No. She had put that behind her and had come here to try a new lifestyle. Church belonged to her Empton life, not her Cape Cod life. Besides, she had agreed to work today. There might not be an evening service to go to when she got done.

She would phone home later and see how they all were, say hello. Then her mother was sure to ask where Muffie—Martha—had gone to church and Muffie would have to say she hadn't gone and. . .

She wouldn't call. She'd write.

The persistent church bell was still pealing as she went up the apartment stairs. Bree was up and dressed, ready to go. She was "on" today too. Maybe someday Muffie would get to the beach, but it wouldn't be possible today because she would be working at the information desk. Besides, she didn't like beaches in the hot sun. She didn't tan; she burned and freckled. She liked beaches in the early morning and the evening.

Bree was still sleepy but beginning to chat in her fast, funny patter, picking up momentum as she came more and more awake. Rather quiet herself and from a quiet family, Muffie found this habit amusing and annoying by turns, alternately wishing she too had the gift of small talk and that she could have a little quiet now and then. She had solved this dilemma by disappearing to solitude occasionally. The rest of the time, she enjoyed the chatter.

Bree was now on the subject of Charlie, and Muffie only half listened as she hurried to change into her uniform.

"Let's go to work," Muffie said, flicking a comb through her curls.

Bree said, "You haven't answered me."

"You can ask me in the car," said Muffie, holding the door open.

"So?" asked Bree, as the Chevy pulled away from the curb. "What do you think of Charlie?"

"Big," said Muffie.

"Oh yes," agreed Bree. "Definitely big. And gorgeous. Don't you think he's gorgeous?"

"I suppose so," said Muffie.

"You *suppose* so!" Bree was shocked. "You ought to see him in his bathing suit. That man is impressive! He can rescue me anytime."

"He certainly has the muscle for it," said Muffie, thinking of the way he had lifted her from the car.

"He likes you, Muffie. I can tell. You just might have a good chance to snag him for the whole summer, if you work it right."

Muffie laughed. "What makes you think I want to snag him?"

"You're a fool if you don't. Half the girls on the beach are in love with him. He can go out with anybody he wants. Always could, I guess. All he has to do is walk by and smile, and they'll follow him all the way to Boston."

Muffie considered. "It takes more than muscle to make a man," she said.

"It's a good start," said Bree. "Major man in college, four years on the football team, fraternity man—like out of the movies. There's nothing wrong with his looks. Or his money—he's got plenty of it. And he's fun. He's always doing something or going someplace. Never a dull moment with Charlie around."

"That's true," said Muffie, thinking that some of those moments were *too* exciting.

"Yeah," said Bree, wistfully.

Muffie shot an appraising glance at her and said, "You sound like you are a little fond of him yourself."

Bree laughed awkwardly. "Yeah. Well, we went 'round

together a couple of summers ago, but after that he kind of moved on. Charlie has a new girl every summer. Then I met Jack and well. . .Jack's a nice guy. We get along pretty well together. He likes me; he wants to get serious, get married, but that's not for me. I want a good time for a few more years before I get stuck with dust and diapers. That's about the only thing we really argue about."

They rode in rare silence for a while before Bree began to talk again, this time about their trip to P'town the night before. She laughed over the raw clams, declaring Muffie to be a good sport. She offered tidbits about the social life there and toyed with the idea of returning to buy a pair of silver earrings she'd seen in one of the arcade shops. Eventually she mentioned the professor.

"Aha," she said, looking sharply at Muffie, "Your interest perked up when I mentioned the professor, didn't it?"

"I'm just listening. That's all," said Muffie.

"You listened like crazy to his conversation last night, too," Bree said, looking wise. "You hung on his words like whales were the thrill of the world."

"I did not."

"You did so."

"Well, the whales sounded interesting. I've never seen one except in pictures and I don't know much about them. It was entirely new to me and I'd like to find out more. Maybe I'll go out on that boat and take a look."

"At the whales or at the professor?"

"At the whales, of course," said Muffie.

"Uh-huh," answered Bree. "Sure. But let me warn you about the professor. First of all, he's dull. He chases whales all day and studies all night. Lots of girls have been fascinated by him and his big blue eyes, but the only thing he cares about is those whales. If you had a spout and fins he might be interested in you, but as it is, you're just one of the crowd. And he's old. He must be at least thirty-five, maybe even older."

"I'll remember that," said Muffie, thinking thirty-five wasn't so hopelessly old.

"Do that. And stick to Charlie. You'll have a lot more fun. By the way, Charlie said for you to be ready at eight tonight. He's taking you out to eat."

"This is the first I've heard of it." Muffie was indignant. "You tell Charlie I said that if he wants to take me out, he can ask me."

"You can tell him yourself when we pick you up."

"We'll see," said Muffie to herself.

"What?"

"Nothing."

Muffie was at the desk for most of the day, answering questions and offering copies of *Summer Sandings*, the Cape Cod National Seashore newspaper, which listed activities. She felt comfortable behind the counter and felt good about the day.

She had forgotten to bring lunch. She thought about dashing out at noon for a quick sandwich, but she was still a stranger to the area and didn't care to hunt about for an uncrowded place. Bree would spend her lunch break (without food) at the beach, working on her tan, so Muffie could go there, just to get away from the desk for a while, but that didn't appeal to her. Charlie would be on the beach and she had a mental picture of him strolling up and down with bikini-clad girls following him as a tail follows a comet. She decided to avoid that scene. Instead, she walked along the path that led to the salt marsh.

The sharp yellow-green of the grasses and the constant chatter of birds filled her with a summer kind of pleasure. She inhaled the air, pungent with an awful smell, possibly rotten. Then, as she got accustomed to it, the smell intrigued her. It was unique, entirely its own smell. She sniffed and listened and watched, trying to memorize smell, sounds, and sights. Before she got enough of this strange atmosphere, her time was gone and she had to hurry back to the Visitors' Center.

The afternoon was so busy that it was closing time before she knew it. At 5:45 she helped close up and by six she was out the door. Bree would be going home with Jack, so Muffie was on her own for a couple of hours until she had to be ready to go out with Charlie.

Had to be ready? What was she thinking? He hadn't even asked her out. He had sent word with Bree, telling—not asking, telling—her to be ready to go out for dinner at eight. He'd ordered her like he'd order a hamburger. It was a wonder he hadn't told her what to wear. Who did she think he was?

He knew who he was—the hero on the beach. *Maybe*, she reflected, *if you're important enough, you don't have to follow the rules other people play by. Maybe. But what arrogance!*

Although, to be fair, he wasn't arrogant when he was with her—just different. And demanding. Definitely demanding. Like a spoiled child.

"It's not really his fault," she said to the hot car as she turned the key in the starter.

Maybe I'll go, she thought. *Bree seems to think Charlie is worth it. I shouldn't be so stuffy that I pass up the fun side of life just because I wasn't properly invited to it. On the other hand, it can't be good for Charlie to have every-body do what he wants. Someone should treat him like an ordinary mortal.*

She thought it over as she drove north toward Wellfleet. Then, on impulse, she turned right, down an unfamiliar road flanked by scrubby little pines set in sandy soil. She followed it up and down hills and around bends until it ended at a crossroad. She turned left, for no particular reason, and found herself on a road paralleling the dunes next to the sea.

For a long time she drove aimlessly, stopping once near a small lake, where she pulled off the road next to a mass of wild pink roses and sat watching families enjoying the water. Another time she parked in a beach lot; leaving the car to stand on a bluff high above the beach, she looked out over the Atlantic, peering toward the horizon as if she could see England out there if she looked hard enough.

From up high, the sea looked more vast than it did from the edge of the foamy wavelets. Children down below played along the edge, chasing the gentle little waves. It was hard to imagine those waves destroying a large ship in a matter of days or less, but she knew they could. A ship-wrecked man might last only a few minutes.

Standing there she felt insignificant, puny, and power-less. "What is man, that thou art mindful of him?" The familiar words of the eighth Psalm came to her unbidden but with new meaning, as though she hadn't really under-stood them until now.

Across that ocean were places she had only read about, ways of life stranger and more exciting than hers. *The world is a magnificent place*, she thought, *and I've seen so small a share of it. How can I go back to my little world?* Ahead

of her stretched day after day of blackboards and atten-
dance, one day indistinguishable from the other, years of
evenings with Ewald. Once this one summer of adventure
was over, she must go back to that life.

"I can't," she said to the ocean, but only the roar of the
waves and the cries of the gulls answered.

You can and you will, she told herself. *It's a good, secure life. And you love to teach. Be grateful for what you
have.*

She sighed.

Her watch said seven-thirty. Charlie'd be at the apartment in half an hour. She'd better get going.

Instead she sat down on the sand at the top of the bank
overlooking the sea. *I should hurry*, she thought, motion-
less. *You're throwing it all away*, she argued with herself,
but she stretched out her long slender legs toward the sea
and scrunched more comfortably into the sand.

A small boy and a man, perhaps his father, got out of a
car nearby. The boy pranced and hopped about, reaching
to touch the kite his father carried. She watched them ready
the yellow-and-blue delta and throw it into the winds atop
the dune. It steadied and held its place above her, growing
small as they let out more string.

She checked her watch. *If I go now, I can just make it*,
she thought. She looked up at the kite again where it hung,
painted on the sky, as steady as Charlie had said deltas
would be. It wasn't moving. Neither was she.

At eight she thought, *He's about there. If I go now, my
lateness will show him that I object to the way he set this
up, but I can still go out with him. Maybe it's not too late*.
She stood, brushed the sand off her uniform, and hurried
to the car.

At her apartment there was no sign of Charlie, no note on the door.

What did you expect? she asked herself. *Did you think he would sit down on your doorstep and wait for you? Him? The golden boy from the beach? You wanted to show him you're as important as he is and now you're stuck here alone. Serves you right.*

The apartment was empty and hot and messy. It smelled of not-quite-clean cabinets, stale crackers, and inferior plumbing. She could hear the drip, drip of the shower. She sat in the middle of the mess on one of the laden chairs, crushing a week's worth of Bree's clothing. She stared at her shoes. *Now what?*

There was no "now what." There was only Sunday evening alone in a hot room in a strange town. She wished Bree were there. Bree always had ideas of things to do. Muffie could imagine what Bree would have to say about this.

Well, no point in staying in these hot rooms, she decided. She might as well get cleaned up and go out for a bite to eat on her own. She might even find something to do. There was a program on whales tonight at the Visitors' Center, but that was about to begin at 8:30, just as she had been telling people all day.

She'd find something. A shower and fresh clothes would make her feel better and then she'd see what she could do.

What she did was walk. The little Lighthouse Restaurant was open, so she ate there and strolled around picturesque Wellfleet. At three hundred years old, the town was still young and alive. Although some houses leaned a bit and some shops were uneven or in need of repair, its quaint old buildings were still in use. Residents continued the fishing trade as Wellfleeters, whale fleeters, had throughout most of its history. Wellfleet oysters were still famous.

New mixed compatibly with the old. Artists had carved out a place in the community and had brought a fame of their own kind to the little town. Paintings and pottery, along with homey crafts like candle making and quilting, drew crowds of discerning and casual browsers to the village, making it a center for the arts and crafts.

At ten o'clock on this Sunday night, people still wandered about, and she felt quite comfortable alone. It wasn't exciting, but it was pleasant, much better than an evening in the room.

By the time she returned, she felt better. Annoyance with her own foolishness had given way to regret and embarrassment. She'd handled the whole thing badly. She knew that now. It would have been better if she'd been there and told him how she felt instead of trying to make her point by her absence. Next time she saw him, she would explain.

In front of her house was Jack's car and sticking out of it were four heads, two close together in the front seat and two even closer in the back seat. On careful inspection she recognized Jack and Bree in front. The two back seat heads moved, and the light from the street lamp caught them. One head, the one with the long dark hair, she had not seen before. The other was Charlie's.

She hoped they wouldn't notice her, but they did. Jack saw her first, acknowledging her presence with a discreet waggle of his fingers, a private greeting that said he realized she'd rather not be seen. Then Bree called her name and added, "What happened to you?"

"Hello," Muffie ventured, as casually as she could. "Hello, Charlie."

"Hi." He didn't seem surprised to see her nor particularly interested. At least, he wasn't interested enough to let go of the brunette, who was now looking resentfully at Muffie. Muffie must have been an unwelcome interruption.

She saw no point in prolonging this awkwardness. She kept on walking, starting across the yard.

"Muffie," called Charlie. She stopped and turned to listen. "Sorry I couldn't keep our date tonight. I had other commitments." His voice didn't sound sorry. The dark-haired girl giggled.

Muffie said nothing. She couldn't think of anything to say. She climbed the stairs and entered the dark apartment without looking back, although from the top of the stairs she thought she heard the car door slam.

"That man!" she muttered to herself. "That egotistical, arrogant ape. Who does he think he is!"

Leaving the apartment light off, she went to stare out the window at the car. It was driving off. The door opened and Bree burst in.

"What's the matter with you!" Bree demanded loudly. "Do you know what you've done?"

Muffie didn't answer, so Bree went on to tell her, in full detail. The gist of it, made short, was that Muffie had ruined her chance with Charlie.

"Not only that," Bree finished, a long time later, "but now he's mad at me for fixing him up with you. I do you a favor and you cause me trouble. Some friend!"

"I'm sorry," said Muffie, "but—"

"But nothing. Any girl in her right mind would jump at the chance to go out with Charlie. He asks you to dinner and you don't show up because you don't like the way he asks you. Stupid. That's what it is. Stupid."

"But—"

"Do you know how long it took him to get another date? Do you? Five minutes, that's how long." Bree went on and on about the other girl.

Now and then, when she could get the word in, Muffie said, "But—" That's as much as she could say before Bree started in again. At last her patience gave way.

"All right! That's enough." Muffie cut through the barrage of Bree's words. "You've been telling me how stupid I am for long enough. Now you listen. I'm sorry if this caused you trouble, but I really don't think it matters that much to Charlie or to Jack. By tomorrow it won't matter to anyone but me.

"Maybe I should have been here, ready to go out like you said, and maybe not. I'm not used to being told secondhand about my dates. I don't like it." Muffie paused before adding, quietly, "I'm also not used to anyone like Charlie."

Bree's anger had passed as she listened. At this last she said, with the ring of personal experience in her voice, "Nobody is, honey. Only Charlie is used to Charlie." Then Bree laughed. "On the other hand, I'll bet Charlie isn't used to anyone like you, either. You should've seen how mad he was. You must be the first woman he ever met that he couldn't control with a snap of his fingers. He may never recover. It was almost worth this mess just to see it." She laughed again.

"You can laugh," said Muffie. "You've got all kinds of

friends around here. I haven't."

Bree said, "You just wait till it gets around that you stood Charlie Cooper up. Everybody will want to meet you, if only to find out if you're really crazy."

Muffie groaned. "Don't tell anybody. Please? It would only embarrass Charlie."

A juicy bit of news like this was prime stuff on the gossip circuit and Bree hated to waste it, but at last she agreed to keep it quiet and to ask Jack to do the same. "Only you have to tell me what Charlie says to you next time."

"There won't be a next time," said Muffie, and she went grimly to bed.

She was wrong. Next time was the next day. Muffie was standing behind the information counter when Charlie came in. She saw him immediately. He blocked so much light in the doorway that there was no way to miss him. Just as quickly, she knew he had seen her. She thought of taking refuge in the office, but since he was part of the staff, just as she was, he would have followed her there. She had no choice but to stay where she was and face his wrath.

"I thought I'd find you here," he growled.

Not if I'd known you were coming, she thought, but what she said was, "About last night—"

"Yeah," he said. "That's what I wanted to see you about. Jack says maybe you didn't understand."

"Maybe I didn't," Muffie said.

"Didn't you get my message?"

"I got it."

"Then where were you?" he demanded.

"Someplace else. Anyway, you said you had another commitment."

Charlie ignored this reference to his parting shot from the evening before. He said, sounding genuinely puzzled, "I thought you wanted to go out with me."

She said, "I thought if you wanted to go out with me you'd have asked me, not sent me an order by way of messenger. I'm not used to being treated like that."

"I'm not used to begging for dates," he snapped.

"I know. You whistle and the girls come running."

"But you don't."

"I don't. If you want a date with me, you'll have to ask me."

"Don't hold your breath, babe."

"And don't call me babe."

Charlie looked at her in disbelief and anger. He towered over her, big enough to snap her in half and looking as if he'd like to.

She stood her ground, grateful for the counter between them. She gave him as steady and calm a look as she could manage. She wondered if he could see that she was shaking right down to her knees.

He sized her up, seeing 124 pounds of offended dignity, matching him look for look, nerve for nerve. He shook his head and slammed his meaty hand down on the counter with a crash.

She jumped, but her look never wavered.

He shook his head again, turned on his heel, and stamped out.

She exhaled slowly, feeling flattened.

"Wow," said Mary Lou, coming out of the office. "What was that all about?"

"He doesn't like my attitude," said Muffie.

"Wow," said Mary Lou again.

Definitely wow, thought Muffie, turning to a somewhat astonished middle-aged man who had been standing there watching. She smiled, although it took effort, and said, "May I help you?"

Good old steady Martha, she thought to herself. *A Muffie would have enough sense to cry.*

four

Charlie sent no more messages and appeared no more at the Visitors' Center. No one else showed interest in spending time with her, either. It was like she had the plague. Or maybe like she *was* the plague. In the social vacuum that followed Charlie's appearance at the Visitors' Center, Muffie had plenty of time to reconsider her actions. She replayed them like a tape in her mind until she had nearly worn this mental tape out. She decided she had been wrong on Sunday night, but that on Monday, in the Visitors' Center, she had been as reasonable and calm as she could manage. No matter who was right or wrong, Charlie was gone and so was the fun he had promised.

Bree rode around in the car with Jack. The others on the staff, seasonal and permanent, paired off very quickly. By the end of her second week, the temporary social structure of summer had been established and the crowd, without Muffie, were packing their free time with parties, picnics, and other social events.

She wasn't entirely left out. General all-staff invitations naturally included her. However, there were no invitations for her specifically. No one asked her out and no one showed special interest. Even the other girls lunched without her unless she pushed her way into their group, and she didn't often do that. Most of the seasonals were younger than she, many in college, so it was possible her age had something to do with it. She also suspected that her friction with Charlie had intimidated virtually every other male who might have asked.

At first Bree offered to find someone else for her, but Muffie steadily refused rather than feel like an ugly duckling who had to accept whatever she could get. Even if she *was* an ugly duckling, she didn't want to feel like one.

And Charlie? He was doing fine with the little brunette. Gossip said Anita had won him for the summer. Gossip also acknowledged that it was only for the summer. Charlie was not interested in serious involvement. For that matter, Charlie didn't seem interested in anything serious.

That was the trouble, Muffie decided. She should not have insisted on behaving like a serious Martha instead of a fluffy Muffie. This was her chance at fun, her vacation to remember. Ha! What it looked like now was just a job away from home.

Home looked better and better. At least there she had some value, even if it was only for being reliable and useful. She had a family who loved her, and friends, and church. And there was always Ewald Phipps.

"Yuk," she said to the piles of Bree's clothing—yuk to the clothing and yuk to Ewald Phipps.

Do something, she thought. What would a Muffie do? A Muffie would find people and join them. On vacation a Muffie would do whatever vacationers do. A Muffie would have a good time no matter what. Would a Muffie attend the evening program called "Portrait of a Coast?" Probably not, but that was the only thing Muffie could find to do on Monday evening, and it was a start.

By eight-thirty the seats in the small indoor auditorium were more than half taken, probably most of them by campers who were glad to be anywhere indoors, out of the drizzle that had started midafternoon. She had never been in a wet tent, but it sounded depressing. She looked around for familiar faces and recognized two who had asked her about the program earlier that day. They seemed not to recognize her out of uniform.

The ranger who introduced the film was a graduate student she knew only slightly. From the film itself she expected very little, so she was pleasantly surprised. She watched as tides and currents and storms changed the coastline, and she found herself caught up in the influence of humankind on this change. She liked the film and liked learning and went home more satisfied with her evening than she had been with the last several evenings.

So the next night she went to the next program. This one, as she told people all day, was on "Whale Strandings." She didn't know this speaker, who was not a ranger but a naturalist with the nearby Massachusetts Audubon Society Sanctuary. His approach was different, more secure, more mature. Experience made the difference, she supposed—that and his huge fund of information.

She watched the slides with interest, appalled by the number of whales lying on the grassy beach. In slide after slide they lay there, dying in spite of the efforts of would-be rescuers to return them to the sea. Although some were saved, most died. A close-up of slicker-clad workers showed concerned faces, intense purpose. One man, a tall, thin one—

Stop, she wanted to say. *I think that's*— But the slides went on before she could be sure that the tall man in the shabby windbreaker was the professor.

Wait, there he is again.

"It's the professor." Fortunately her words were soft and

the background music covered them. She thought, *I'm sure that's him. I recognize those lean gesturing hands. Maybe he'll be in some more slides.*

She missed the rest of the lecture. She was too busy watching for the professor. There were no more pictures of him, none that she recognized anyway, and none of those had shown what she wanted to see. The slides were too far away, too impersonal. Maybe. . .

By the next morning she had decided to go on the whale lab boat. If tourists went on whale sightings, she would go too. Thursday was her day off so, following Bree's instructions, she telephoned from work for a reservation for Thursday morning on the *Minke II* out of Provincetown.

The professor had said to let him know, anytime, but Muffie didn't do that. She figured he had probably forgotten all about her by now, and she felt uncomfortable pushing herself on him. She would buy a ticket like the other tourists and if she happened to run into him, fine.

Thursday was clear and hot, a perfect beach day. Dressing for the temperature, Muffie donned cool slacks and a light sleeveless shirt.

"You'll freeze," said Bree, pointing out that the temperature out in the bay was likely to be several degrees below what it was on the sidewalk in the middle of Wellfleet. The blouse wasn't right, according to Bree, and neither were the shoes. The pants would do, but wouldn't the blue ones be better? Especially with the soft blue blouse with the little anchor on the pocket?

"What difference does it make?" argued Muffie. "The whales don't care what I look like."

"You never know who you'll run into," said Bree, nodding wisely.

Whom, thought Muffie, but she didn't say it because Muffies don't worry about grammar.

Bree fussed and selected and Muffie did what she was told until Bree stepped back satisfied. "Here, take my blue slicker," said Bree, snatching it from the bottom of the pile on the sofa and pressing it under Muffie's arm. "You'll look like a New England fisherman."

Muffie protested that the slicker was hot and that it was not raining and that she didn't want it and that she had a tan raincoat of her own and that it was too much trouble to carry and that it probably wouldn't fit. Besides, don't fishermen wear yellow slickers? Nevertheless, when Muffie left, she carried the blue slicker over her arm.

Driving in Provincetown was only a little easier on Thursday mornings than it was on Saturday nights. All the parking places on the streets were full, but the big lot on Macmillan Pier was still open. She parked there and locked the car, reaching in for Bree's blue slicker at the last minute because she knew Bree would ask later.

Macmillan Pier was large enough to support several shops and a restaurant. It reached out from the center of town into the bay and ended abruptly in a large building. The *Minke II* ticket booth was about halfway down the pier, on her right, just as Bree had said, and the *Minke II* itself was tied alongside. About a dozen people had already formed the beginnings of a line for boarding, and others came immediately after she got in line.

On board the boat, which was about ten times bigger than she had pictured, several young people moved and straightened things and otherwise prepared for the trip. Their ages and attitudes reminded her of the seasonal rangers. They were youngish, relaxed, and good-humored and went about their tasks with easy competence.

None of these people was the professor. Perhaps this was not his boat after all. Or perhaps this was his day off. She felt unaccountably disappointed, although she would have hastened to assure Bree that she hadn't come to see him particularly and really had no reason to expect him to be there. If she had wanted to see him, she would have let him know she was coming, wouldn't she? At the same time she was both disappointed and surprised that she was disappointed.

On the back deck were work tables and unfamiliar charts. Ahead of that the center of the boat was enclosed, with benches on the inside and a counter that offered minimal snacks.

It was stuffy in there, so she stepped outside on the wide open deck that ran along the entire length of the boat on each side. She found a place on one of the benches attached to the outside wall of the enclosed section and sat. Then, restless and curious, she rose again to explore the front of the boat, where crew members were handling ropes and making ready to sail. They cast the lines off and pushed away. The boat shifted direction. The light breeze stiffened to a gust and then became a steady wind in her face. Some announcement came over the loudspeakers, but she could barely hear it. Other passengers were moving to the back of the boat. She followed.

On the rear deck a young man was introducing himself as a naturalist with a special interest in whales and was offering to provide information that might make their trip more profitable. She listened as he touched on the major kinds of whales and told them that if they were lucky, they would see whales close up, probably humpback whales, or the less commonly seen Minke. If they were really fortunate, they might even be able to recognize particular whales by the markings on their flukes, their huge tail flippers, since these marks are known to be as individual in whales as fingerprints are in humans. Some of the crew knew these great whales by name and would identify them over the loudspeaker if they could.

The rough, light brown, woodlike material in his hand was baleen, the substitute for teeth in certain types of whales. He demonstrated the way the whale took in huge mouthfuls of water and let it run out again through the baleen, straining out (or in, in this case) small organisms in the water. These it ate, feeding on small animals, although it could easily have swallowed large fish whole.

Or a man, she thought, remembering Jonah. She thought of him as she held the piece of baleen for closer inspection. To a whale, little Jonah would have been only one bite. Less.

The small chart she received with pictures of the different kinds of whales, so that she could identify them, was a puzzle. These whales didn't look the way they were supposed to look. Most of them had low, concave foreheads instead of the great smooth domed heads she usually saw on tieclip whales and storybook covers.

"When you've seen one whale, you've seen 'em all," Charlie had said. Evidently Charlie was wrong. She must have read about these different whales somewhere, but somehow the specifics had escaped her.

Would she be able to identify a particular whale? She doubted it, unless the whale came completely out of the water so she could get a look at its whole shape, and that was not the least likely. She folded the chart and stuffed it

into the slicker pocket and, now that the boat was under-
way, went to find a place on the long side benches, near the
middle in the sun, where she could watch the water and
peer out toward the horizon in search of whale spouts. The
wind was stronger and colder, and the air smelled different
in some way she couldn't explain. It smelled like the sea,
she supposed, with some special qualities belonging only
to the sea.

As the *Minke II* rounded the point of Cape Cod and moved
out into the deeper waters of the bay, the water grew much
rougher. The waves slapped the sides of the boat and threw
sea spray into the air, wetting those people unfortunate
enough to be standing in the wrong place at the wrong
time. Most people went inside.

Muffie put on the slicker, grateful for its dry warmth
and the independence it gave her. As spray spattered the
slicker, she pulled up the hood and snuggled into it.

"Mind if I join you?"

The voice was familiar and so were the sea blue eyes.
For a moment she saw nothing else but those eyes. Then,
slowly, she gathered awareness and the pleasure of seeing
him. She moved over to make a little more room, although
there was plenty, and he sat.

"I came to see your whales," she said, looking out at the
horizon.

They—really, he—spoke of whales for the next half hour
or more as they cruised to Stahlwagon Banks, where whales
frequently gathered. Basic stuff to him was new and exciting to her. His enthusiasm was contagious, and she found
she was even more fascinated with whales than she had
been when she'd first listened to him talk with Jack.

Gradually the conversation changed slightly to an explanation of his studies of the cetacean population, and she was struck again by his intensity. Some of what he said was obscure to her, some of his vocabulary too technical. She didn't ask what the words meant; she just listened, savoring his joy in his work.

A shout from the pilot's cabin above them interrupted his stream of talk. "Over there!" shouted a man nearby.

"A whale has been sighted on the left, about ten o'clock position," said the voice on the loudspeaker.

The professor pointed and Muffie looked, but she saw nothing. Squinting against the sun, she stared at the horizon, not blinking for fear of missing the whale. In the distance she saw only the sea and the sky and the birds that circled and dived from one element to the other.

"Closer," said the professor, pulling her to stand at the railing and pointing to the water about forty feet from the boat.

As she stared, a gray curved shape broke the surface of the water and spouted. She gasped. Again it surfaced, closer. No, it was a second one. Two, both at the surface, closer, closer, then right next to the boat. By leaning over the railing, she could see that one was much larger than the other.

"A baby," she said, grasping the professor's forearm.

"That's probably Melissa and her calf," he said, looking oddly at her hand on his arm. His other hand hovered over her hand as if to light on it and cover it, but unconscious of this, she pulled her hand away to reach toward the whale.

He cleared his throat. "She brings her baby to us to amuse it, I think, the way we take our children to watch the monkeys in the zoo. Mothers with calves often approach our boat. Watch now; she may sound. You might get a glimpse of her flukes and we can verify her identity."

More of the huge gray back appeared and then disappeared. Her enormous flukes rose to stand at right angles to the surface of the water and vanish into it with little splash.

"M," said Muffie, reading a letter made by the blaze of white on the underside of the fluke.

"Exactly. 'M' for Melissa," he said. "Excuse me." He left her standing in the sea spray, watching for another whale.

Altogether she saw six more whales up close and sighted another dozen farther off—more than that, counting spout sightings. Those watching on the other side of the boat saw some of the same and some different whales. There was no bad place to stand except inside.

The loudspeaker announced too soon that they must return to shore. She stood at her place by the railing, straining her eyes to see for a long time after the *Minke II* turned in a large half circle and headed for port, but she saw no more whales. Unwilling to go in, she resumed her seat on the bench and scanned the waves, just in case she saw a spout.

"Magnificent," she said to the sea.

"Yes," said the professor, "they are magnificent."

"Oh," she said, startled. "I didn't know you were there. I was just—"

"Talking to yourself?" He smiled. "I do it all the time. That way I know somebody's listening, even if it's only me listening to myself."

She looked sharply at him to see if he was laughing at her. He wasn't. Not at all.

"You were telling me about your weekly helicopter flight

over the water to maintain a whale census," she said, hoping he would pick up where he had left off.

He did. He was still enthusiastically explaining whale migrations to her when the *Minke II* bumped the dock gently and tied up. He stopped then, although it was clear that he could have gone on for quite a while.

She stood uncertainly and held out her hand. "Thank you," she said and smiled up at him.

He took her hand. "I'm afraid I've bored you," he said, still holding her hand.

"Not at all," she said. "I enjoyed it. It was the loveliest day I've had since I've been on Cape Cod."

"It's only half a day," he pointed out, "and you haven't had lunch. How about sharing mine—that is, if you don't think Charlie will object."

"He won't," she said as she pulled her hand free. "Charlie and I aren't—I'd love to share your lunch."

He looked at her curiously, but she said no more. He followed her up the gangplank and walked along slowly with her to the beach where she and Charlie had flown the kite.

"Wait here," he said. "I'll get lunch."

She found a place on the sand away from the walkers and swimmers and settled down where she could watch people come and go on the pier. The sun was hot on the blue slicker, so she took it off and spread it out for a picnic table.

Good thing I have it, she thought as she smoothed the flattering blue shirt and pants Bree had insisted she wear. Bree must have known it would be cold out there. Bree must also have guessed she might see the professor. Bree seemed to know these things.

Soft, sandy footsteps behind were a warning before the shadow fell across the slicker. "Ah, Professor. Back already?" she said, looking up. But it wasn't the professor. "Charlie!"

"Bree said you'd be here," Charlie said.

She had no words. He folded himself down to sit across from her and waited.

Finally she said, "Yes?"

"Yes," he answered. "Well, Jack says—I mean maybe I—um, about that last time we met—"

"Yes," she said, then out of pity for his struggle to say the right thing, she added, "Let's forget it."

"Right," he said, looking uncertain but much relieved. "Listen, I'm on lunch break, and I have hardly any time. I came to ask what you're doing Saturday night. I mean, would you like to go to the party with me Saturday? It's not really a staff party—just some of the gang."

"What happened to Anita?"

"Never mind Anita. Would you or wouldn't you?"

"I would like to go out with you Saturday, Charlie. Thank you for asking," she said, very formally.

"Don't overdo it," he said. "We'll pick you up at eight. Okay?"

"Eight would be fine," she said.

"Right. Hello, Professor," Charlie said, looking over Muffie's head and rising to his feet.

The two men exchanged chilly greetings before Charlie strode off in the direction of the parking lot. She expected the professor to comment on Charlie's unexpected appearance, but he didn't. He only looked at her questioningly. She shrugged, and he seemed to accept that as her answer.

She helped him unpack the lunch—ham and cheese sandwiches and lemonade for two—the same food she had been eating the night they first met. *Observant of him*, she thought, and wondered what else he had noticed.

She unwrapped her sandwich and raised it to her lips before she realized that he was waiting. To her astonishment, he bowed his head and said grace over their little lunch.

"You're surprised," he said, when he finished.

She said, "I didn't expect it. I thought I left that behind me in Indiana."

He said, "I don't usually pray in public like this either. I like to keep my prayers for places and ears that are open to them. With you it felt right."

She blushed and nervously began to talk about home and her family and the Christian atmosphere in which she had been raised. He was a good listener, making her feel that what she said really mattered. The lunch was long gone when at last she came to a stop.

"I've talked and talked," she said. "I've told you all about me and you've told me all about whales and I really should be going. Thanks for the lunch, and thanks for listening, Professor."

"Adam," he said.

"Adam," she repeated.

He walked her to the lot where her car sat baking in the sun.

"If you really want to know more about whales, you might like to visit the little historical museum in town here sometime," he suggested. "It's not exactly a whaling museum, but since this is an old whaling town, there's quite a bit about whaling in the museum."

"I would," she said.

"Now?"

She tossed the slicker into the back seat and relocked the car. "Now," she said.

They walked down Commercial Street to the little white frame building set on a slight rise above street level. "Why, it's an old church," she said.

"That's not so strange," he answered. "It's only natural that whaling communities need their churches. They are very much aware of God, these whalers and their families, and all 'They that go down to the sea in ships, that do business in great waters; These see the works of the Lord, and his wonders in the deep.'"

"Psalms?" she ventured.

"Psalm 107," he confirmed. "God feels very close out there on the sea." He fell silent and she left him to his thoughts as they wandered upstairs and down, through the exhibits of the little museum.

The silence between them was comfortable, companionable, with no feeling that the silence must be filled in with words in order to keep the link between them. Muffie was very aware of that link. It intruded on her thoughts, dominated them, until the main thing she saw in the museum was Adam.

At the door they both hesitated.

"The Pilgrim Monument might still be open," he said slowly.

"I really—"

"You've seen it," he said.

"No, but really—"

"You're right. There's not enough time to do it properly. The exhibit on whaling is really very fine. The scrimshaw is—I'm sorry. I get so involved in whales and whaling that

I forget that other people aren't."

"Now that I've seen a whale up close, I think I can understand," she said.

He studied her for a long moment before giving a slight nod that might or might not indicate approval. "I believe you do understand," he finally said.

She began again, "I really must go. It's been a fascinating day—a wonderful day—but I think I've taken too much of your time away from your work. I don't want you to be sorry I came."

"I'm not," he said.

They walked slowly back toward the parking lot. As they passed the raw bar, she told him about her first clam on the half shell, laughing at herself when she told how cautious she had been and how she hadn't wanted to try it.

"Why did you, if you didn't want to?" he asked.

"I had to," she said. "I can't spend all my life being afraid of trying new things. Not if I'm going to live the life I want to live. Not if I'm going to fit in with Bree and, well. . ."

"Charlie," he finished.

"Yes, and Charlie," she said, wondering why she felt defensive about saying it.

"What if you never fit with them?"

"I will."

"What if you don't?"

"I will. I do."

He said nothing more. *I do fit*, she thought. *I have no doubts. Not really. Not after today when Charlie actually tried to apologize and ask me out in spite of his anger. Charlie must like me and he must think I fit. Still. . .*

"I've offended you," Adam said, breaking into her

thoughts.

She said, "No. I just think you're wrong."

He said, "Maybe I am. I hope not."

They walked the rest of the way in awkward silence.

"Thanks," she said again as she rolled down her car window from inside the hot car. She started the engine.

He put a hand on the burning hot window sill and quickly jerked his hand away. He leaned down to say, "Would you like to see the Pilgrim Monument, maybe next Thursday afternoon when I finish the morning sighting trip?"

She smiled and nodded. "I'll be here about three."

"Make it one. I'll buy you a ham sandwich and tell you about whales."

She nodded again and he straightened to his full height. She slipped the car into gear and pulled slowly away, watching him shrink in her rearview mirror.

Bree was right. The man was in love with his whales. No doubt she was also right about his having no time for romance, although today he had been friendly, definitely friendly. Bree would say that's all it was. But she had also said the professor was dull, and he wasn't. Not at all. He was fascinating. He listened and understood. He knew things and wanted to know more. Actually, she thought he knew too much sometimes, made her think too much.

He's not at all like Charlie, she told herself. *Maybe it's just that Adam is older, or at least he seems older. He must be over thirty, maybe even thirty-two or thirty-three, but not the thirty-five Bree estimated. To Bree at her young twenty-four, that would seem older than it does to me. To me, thirty-three seems quite a sensible age.*

"Especially for a friend," she said, and then smiled to remember his having caught her talking to herself.

She was still smiling to herself when Bree came in that night.

"Tell me all about it," Bree demanded before she even shut the door.

Muffie looked up from the letter she was writing and gestured at the room in general. "I cleaned," she said, as if that were the subject.

Bree stared around the orderly room. All the furniture was visible and uncluttered. The ironing board stood folded in its corner and their meager supply of food was tidily stashed in plastic containers on one end of the otherwise empty table.

"Your clothes are in there," Muffie added.

They were neatly arranged in more boxes from the grocery and on another rope across the room. Bree glanced quickly at the unaccustomed order.

"Thanks," Bree said. "I was going to do it myself as soon as I got the time. Really."

Muffie nodded.

"But tell me what happened," Bree demanded.

Muffie shrugged with careful casualness. "He's very nice, not dull at all. I like him."

"Of course you like him. Everybody likes him. Tell me, did he actually come up there and ask you for a date?"

"Oh, you mean Charlie. Yes, he did."

"Who did you think I meant?" asked Bree, puzzled for a moment. "Oh, the professor. Yes, he's nice, but tell me exactly what Charlie said, word for word."

Bree sat down and leaned forward to listen. Muffie told her, as well as she could remember, in spite of Bree's frequent interruptions.

"Fantastic!" was Bree's verdict. "I never thought he'd

do it. And it didn't hurt anything to have the professor right there to make him jealous. Pretty neat, if I do say so myself."

"What do you mean?" asked Muffie.

Bree grinned with mischievous pride. "Who do you think planned all this? Did you think the professor just happened to bump into you on the boat, just happened to know you would be there in a blue slicker? And how do you think Charlie knew where to find you?"

"You didn't."

"I did, with a little help from Jack, of course. And some good luck at having them run into each other. You should be grateful. You weren't doing very well on your own."

Muffie's smile disappeared, along with her confidence. "I'm not grateful at all," she said. "I'm embarrassed. They'll think I asked you to do this."

Bree shook her head. "No, they won't. Charlie knows better. He knows you're too stubborn."

"But Adam—"

"Adam? You call him Adam? Well! Maybe I've under-estimated you if the reserved old professor got first-name friendly with you in one afternoon. Nobody else calls him that, except maybe his mother, and I'm not sure she does either. Don't worry about the professor. Jack told him you didn't expect to see him. Besides, I told you before, he's a waste of time unless you're a whale. Stick with Charlie."

"That's what Charlie says," mused Muffie.

"It's good advice. Take it from an expert."

Muffie didn't ask what Bree meant by that last remark. She thought she was probably happier not knowing.

five

For Saturday night's party, Muffie dressed very carefully in the new lavender shirtwaist dress she'd been saving for a special occasion. It fit well, not too tight and not too short. The color suited her too, softening the brightness of her hair and bringing out the whiteness of her skin. She turned in front of the cloudy mirror. *Yes*, she thought, *it's just right*.

But no, Bree didn't think so. "The lavender is too pale and makes you look washed out," she said. "It's too long and baggy—a great dress for an old lady—and worst of all, it looks like something you made yourself."

"I did," Muffie admitted, looking at the dress again and wondering what was wrong with homemade.

So for Saturday night's party, Bree dressed Muffie in Bree's own skin-tight designer jeans and Bree's own backless, shoulderless, sleeveless black-and-silver knit top. Muffie's bone-colored high-heeled sandals were not quite right, but they would have to do. Bree would have preferred black or silver, but at least the high heels were better than the moccasins Muffie seemed determined to wear. Huge silver earring loops completed the gear.

"You need a little more green on your eyelids and just a touch more lipstick," said Bree, applying colors liberally to an impatient model.

When she was at last permitted to see her new image in the mirror, the dressed and redressed Muffie stared at the stranger staring back at her. She squinted and moved closer to see more clearly, but it didn't help. She blinked at the mirror up close, fascinated by the snaky effect of green and silver on her eyelids. *Creepy*, she thought.

"I can't go out in public like this," said Muffie, kicking off the shoes.

"Do you want to be seen or do you want to be ignored?" demanded Bree.

"Ignored," answered Muffie.

"You've already tried that. Now try it my way. If you don't like it, you can always go back to your old—and I do mean *old*—look."

"These pants don't fit. I can't sit down. I can't even bend over very far. And they're too short."

"Perfect," said Bree. "They were too big on me anyway."

Muffie looked at Bree's tight jeans and electric blue bare-midriff top and then looked back at her own reflection. They were dressed much alike, but on Bree the look seemed normal.

"Come on," Bree said. "Don't scowl like that. Charlie will love it. You'll see."

Charlie did love it. He couldn't keep his eyes off her. She tried to avoid his eyes, but there was nowhere else to look. He was everywhere.

"I can't get over it," he said. "Miss Puritan herself, and now she's a rock star. I had you figured all wrong."

"It was Bree's idea," Muffie explained, feeling awkward and miserable. She tried to straighten her right knee where the jeans were cutting into her flesh. There wasn't room. She shifted in the seat and found she had shifted closer to him. She tried to shift back but his arm over her shoulders held her where she was.

"Excuse me," she said, and stretched arms and legs out in a giant fake yawn. She made certain one of her elbows stabbed sharply at his chest and that the sudden motion pushed his arm off her shoulders. She stretched again to make more room. "Claustrophobia," she said.

He grinned and moved away, slightly.

Muffie caught Jack's eye in the rearview mirror long enough to see that Jack was enjoying her maneuvers. He leaned over to whisper something to Bree, who laughed and glanced quickly over the seat at Muffie.

I hate this, thought Muffie.

Pulsing rhythms of heavy drum and augmented electric guitar shook the air as far as a full block away from the party. From the front yard, the sound was aggressive. From the back yard, where the party was in full boom, the music bordered on debilitating. None of the forty or fifty party-goers, a few of them from the staff of the National Seashore, were attempting to dance to the live music. Impossible as it seemed to Muffie, they were engaged in conversation. How could they hear?

"Charlie!" The crowd shouted a general welcome for the life of the party, and he made it include her. She smiled politely as Charlie propelled her to the middle of the largest group. In five minutes Charlie had put a soft drink in her hand and started on his first beer. In ten minutes she had been sized up by every girl there and by several of the nearer men. They were not subtle in their looking, and she was not subtle in the icy reception she gave their stares. In twenty minutes she was alone.

If there were a tray, I could pass it around, she thought, *and that way I would at least be doing something useful.*

There was no tray. She minced toward the house, fighting the jeans all the way, to find the hostess, whom she knew slightly, to offer help.

The kitchen, jammed with talkers and drinkers, was hotter and noisier than the yard. Getting in was difficult. Getting out became essential. As soon as she could slither between incoming guests, she escaped to the relative peace of the outdoors. Looking about for an inconspicuous place, she struggled toward a corner of the porch, where she leaned uncomfortably against the railing and wished the jeans would permit her to sit.

Now and then she could hear Charlie's laughter from the other side of the yard, usually followed by a general burst of hilarity from the crowd that always seemed to be around him. Gradually her ears dulled to the music, and she found she could make out a few voices around her. How long she leaned there listening to snatches of conversation she did not know. It seemed a very long time before an unfamiliar voice said in her ear, "How about another drink?"

"No, thank you."

"Dance?"

She saw that a few couples had begun to dance in the area in front of the little band. She thought they were couples. Since no one was actually touching anyone else, it was hard to tell.

"No, thank you," she said, without explaining that her clothes barely let her walk, much less dance. It didn't matter. She didn't dance anyway.

The owner of the voice pushed his face close to hers and laid one heavy, possessive hand on her shoulder. She could not avoid the sour smell of beer. He said, "Well, then, if you don't want to dance, how about a kiss?"

She pushed his hand off her shoulder. "No, thank you."

Arguing and protesting, he followed her as she moved back into the kitchen, pushing her way into the midst of the throng. She lost him in there somewhere. When she squeezed out the other side, he was gone.

Her ears were beginning to hurt from the weight of the huge silver earrings. She took them off and tried to stuff them in her jeans pocket. It was no use. She put them back on. Now and then she found a girl to talk to, but the conversations didn't last long. The girls were interested in the men and drifted off with them as soon as they could. She had several conversations with men, too, but these didn't last long either.

By ten she had had more than enough. By midnight she was miserable, but the party showed no sign of breaking up. She began to realize that the party would stop when the beer finally ran out. For a wild moment or two she considered dumping the rest of the beer. She could sneak over there to the keg and turn the tap on. The beer would run out onto the yard and that would end the party. It was tempting.

At one a.m., when the band took a break, she discovered that she could still hear drums when the music wasn't being played. On longer reflection she decided that what she was hearing was the thump of her own nervous system as it still reverberated to the attack it had received.

She checked the level of the beer supply again and was relieved to learn that little was left. The hostess made the same discovery and brought out more. Muffie sagged wearily against the side of the porch to wait for the party to end.

She never did see the end of it. At 3:30 Charlie's singing had reached the pitch, or lack of pitch, that proved beyond doubt that he had had more party than he could handle. Jack led him off, still singing, and sent Bree to fetch Muffie. That Bree had been drinking, too, was evident, but Jack seemed as sober as Muffie herself.

It took all three of them to stuff Charlie into the back seat. He just barely fit. Muffie wondered if he had grown since they'd arrived. She pushed his feet over and crowded in next to him. He didn't notice or didn't care. She couldn't tell which.

Jack was quiet at the wheel, but Charlie and Bree sang loudly all the way to the main highway. Muffie vainly attempted to quiet them. They bounced along the twisty road and took one final sharp turn to meet the main highway. The suddenness of the turn threw the extremely relaxed Charlie in her direction and his weight crushed her against the side of the car.

"Hey! Here's little Duffie!"

She didn't correct her name. There wasn't any point. She was simply grateful that he had stopped singing. She thought that would be an improvement. It wasn't. Now that he had discovered her, he reached for her.

"Come here, Fluffie," His arm reached round her and pulled her his direction in spite of the fact that there was no room for her to move. His other hand landed on her knee. She pushed it off and it came right back. She pushed it off again and planted it firmly on his own knee.

He laughed and used that hand to turn her face up to his. "Huffie," he said, and laughed again, filling her nose with beer fumes. "Come on, beautiful, let's have a kiss for Ol' Charlie."

She pulled her chin to free it from his hand, but her chin didn't move. Her hands fighting against his were useless. Against his chest they were nothing. Against his face they were an annoyance, a part of the game, no more than that. His face was next to hers and then his mouth was on hers.

She struggled and kicked and came up fighting. "No!" she shouted. "No! Let me go!"

"Aw, come on, Tuffie. You know you like it. You've been prancin' around in those little tight pants all night just waitin' for Ol' Charlie to get around to kissin' you."

"Get away from me," she threatened.

"Or you'll do what?" He laughed again and tried for another kiss.

She fought him off again. She was much smaller than he and should have realized it was useless, but the fighting came from fear and disgust. He had her solidly pinned against the door, her wrist in his crushing grasp, and she hid her face against his chest in the only protection she could find until the car stopped in front of her apartment.

Jack was out of the car and at her side in a moment. He opened the door and reached in to pry one of Charlie's hands free. In a carefully ordinary tone Jack said, "Easy, Charlie, easy. You'll hurt her. You don't want to hurt Muffie."

"No," said Charlie, slowly changing to a new thought. "Don't want to hurt Muffie."

Jack said, "Let her go, Charlie. She's home."

To Muffie's relief, Charlie did let her go. Jack helped her from the car and asked quietly if she was okay. She nodded.

"You'd better take Bree in," Jack said. "Can you manage?"

Muffie said, "I think so. How will you manage Charlie by yourself?"

"I've done it before," Jack answered. "I'll be okay as long as he doesn't get belligerent. If he wants to fight, I'll let him sleep in the back seat."

"Why do you do this, Jack?" Muffie asked.

Jack shook his head and went back to Charlie.

Once upstairs with the sagging, giggling Bree, Muffie dragged the heavy weight of the small girl onto the bed. She pulled off Bree's high-heeled shoes and left her there. She put water for tea in the small electric hot pot and tried to sit down to wait for it. Sitting was impossible. She changed into cool, loose pajamas and padded barefoot back to the table. *This is crazy*, she thought. *I'm too tired for tea and too upset.*

She unplugged the hot pot and lay down on the sofa. What a night! She was exhausted, drained. More than anything else she could think of right then, she wanted a soothing hot shower. She looked at the clock. Four-thirty. If she took a shower now she'd wake up everyone in the house, except Bree. Nothing would wake Bree. In three more hours she could have her shower.

Shutting Charlie solidly out of her mind, she concentrated on the party, working through it in her mind. She could still hear music in the back of her head, where it seemed to have taken up permanent residence. Maybe it was an age thing, she reflected. Maybe if she were sixteen. . .

Nobody at the party was sixteen. Maybe it wasn't age at all, but some personality difference that made her more comfortable with quiet. Noise had always grated on her. It was only reasonable that extreme noise would be repugnant.

There was something else too, some kind of noise of the spirit that had destroyed her peace, a kind of spiritual static. The guests had seemed desperate in their search for a good time. They had tried too hard. They had talked too loudly, laughed pointlessly, drunk without satisfying thirst. In retrospect she saw them as some kind of imprisoned souls grasping for a taste of pleasure. Especially Charlie. He had grabbed at the noise and the laughter, desperately greedy for it.

I'm tired, she thought. *My imagination is running away with me. They probably had a wonderful time at the party. Jack and Bree seemed to, and Charlie. If I had tried harder, maybe I could have had a good time too.*

No, on second thought she knew she wouldn't. If having a good time meant drinking too much, she was never going to have a good time. It was that simple. Being drunk was repulsive and foolish. She could never allow herself to be like that. Even lovely Bree had lost her grace and her quick wit. What had Jack thought, Muffie wondered, when he'd seen Bree like that, especially since Jack had stayed sober.

She wished Charlie had been sober. She shuddered again at the memory of the struggle in the car. He wouldn't have been that way if he had been sober. Or would he? She didn't know. For the first time it occurred to her that Charlie might have expected her to cooperate in his back seat gropings even if he had been cold sober. He must have pawed dozens of other girls. Had they cooperated? Some of them must have.

Oh, Charlie, she mourned, *beautiful Charlie. Why do you have to be like that?*

She lay there watching leaves move against the window

screen. Expecting them to make a dry, scratching sound, she listened for it. From some place close by, her bird sang, sometimes trilling, sometimes striking single, clear notes. His voice was clear and strong in the night stillness. And very loud.

Now? she thought. *In the middle of the night? I thought birds slept all night, except for owls and such. This songbird should be asleep with his head under his wing. What bird is this?*

She concentrated on the melody, willing away the rude battle with Charlie and the lonely discomfort of the party. As the melody swelled, the party faded. The pounding in her brain eased and her tense muscles relaxed.

"What a blessing you are," she said drowsily to the bird, and fell asleep.

The church bell woke her, or maybe it was habit that made her eyes open. Either way, it was too early and she turned her face to the darkness of the sofa back and tried to go back to sleep. She couldn't.

If she had followed her own natural inclination, she would have bathed, dressed in her best white dress, and gone to church. She rose and moved to do just that, but in the shower the contrast between the party last night and church this morning made her ashamed to go to church. She couldn't face *herself* this morning. How could she face God?

She wasn't due at work until later, but she didn't want to stay around until Bree woke up. She decided to go in to work early, reasoning that she might feel better if she was busy.

It was just as well for the crew on duty that she did go in. Richard definitely was feeling the effects of the party, and at the desk a pale Mary Lou was glad to see her. These two, who had scarcely spoken to her the night before, welcomed her this morning with as much genuine enthusiasm as they could feel over their headaches.

Muffie was glad to be there. If she had stayed home, she would have had too much time to think. She had thought enough last night, more than enough, and now she simply wanted to empty her mind and forget. Besides, she liked to be useful.

Richard didn't look good, so she volunteered to be the guide for the film that ran at intervals in the auditorium. She didn't have to do much but welcome the audience and introduce the film. The auditorium was more than half full when she saw Charlie standing in the right-hand aisle. He gestured to her to meet him outside and she nodded. Once she had the audience settled and the film started, she could slip out the back and meet him.

Did she want to? Absolutely not, but she did want some peace of mind, so she went.

"How do you feel?" she asked in greeting.

"Rotten. How about you?"

"Okay," she said, which was true, if she considered only how she felt physically.

He rubbed the back of his thick neck and looked down at her with what she thought must be embarrassment. It was hard to tell with Charlie. He said, "Listen, about last night.Uh. . .great party, wasn't it?"

"Wild," she said, absolutely without enthusiasm, and wondered why she'd said it.

"I mean, you had a good time, didn't you?"

"Did you, Charlie?"

"Yeah. So how about next Saturday? There's a party over at the beach."

"I don't think so, Charlie. Thanks anyway. I don't think I'm the party type."

"Sure you are. You just need to loosen up and thaw out a little. Once you relax and start to talk to people, you'll be fine. What's wrong?"

The tight jeans were wrong, she thought, *and that ridiculous non-blouse, and those enormous earrings. I tried to fit in and I didn't.* She said, "It's not for me, Charlie. Ask Anita."

"I don't ask Anita; I tell her. You're different. You I ask, so I'm asking. That's what you want, isn't it?"

"Yes."

"So?" he insisted.

She thought. "No," she said finally.

"What kind of answer is that!" Charlie's exasperation was loud in the echoing hallway. She turned away, embarrassed. His huge hand caught her shoulder and spun her around to face him. "What kind of answer is that? Tell me."

She tried to turn, but he held her fast. She looked straight up at him and kept her voice as firm as possible. "Let go of me, Charlie."

He gave her shoulder a little shake and pushed her away, his eyes blurred with confusion, his mouth hard with anger.

"Charlie, I do not want to go to the party with you. I do not like your parties. I do not even like me when I go to them. Okay?" She enunciated each word very distinctly, telling him with her voice what she was not saying with her words.

He stood as though stricken. She knew intuitively that he had almost never been turned down by a girl and that what he was hearing was a shock. *It's about time,* she thought. Charlie ought to learn that other people have feelings too. Just because he was the handsomest man she'd ever seen, with the warmest smile and the most appealing eyes, he didn't have the right to. . .

Right now his eyes looked confused and hurt. *Poor Charlie.* It wasn't his fault she didn't like his parties. She said, "I'm sorry, Charlie. I like you. I really do. It's just that—"

It was the wrong thing to say. Charlie recoiled from her in anger. "Forget it," he growled and stalked off in the direction of the exit. She watched him slam open the door, ignoring the already open door next to it, and disappear.

"Good-bye," she said when he was gone, and strode in the opposite direction, back to the auditorium. *That wretched party,* she thought. *And those clothes! If I had worn the lavender dress the way I wanted to, I wouldn't feel so ashamed.*

Yes, ashamed. She was ashamed of the way she had dressed, practically advertising for those unwelcome advances she had gotten. No wonder those men had thought she wanted them. Her stomach quailed at the memory.

It wasn't Bree's fault. Bree had meant well. Even Muffie recognized that those awful clothes looked like what most of the other girls had worn. The lavender dress would have looked out of place.

It should have looked out of place. I was out of place, she thought. *What was I doing there?*

Trying to have fun, only it wasn't fun, not then and not later and not now. Charlie wouldn't understand that. He couldn't have known that she wouldn't like the party or the music or the beer. Or the back seat struggle.

Her arm, just above the wrist, was bluish where he had bruised it in that struggle. She lightly touched it, feeling the tenderness beneath the skin. She supposed he hadn't realized he had held it so tightly in that crushing grip of his.

He was not going to do that again. That was the last time she would allow him to hurt her like that. If he couldn't control his own behavior, she certainly could control hers. She would simply see to it that she wasn't near him when he had been drinking.

But he liked beer and drank it as she drank water. To avoid him when he drank meant she'd have to avoid him totally.

Okay, she thought. *He won't ask me out again anyway. Fine. He overreacted to the whole thing. I have a right to prefer other kinds of recreation. He's angry over nothing. I'm the one who should be angry. I'm the one who had a boring evening with a rude date who left me alone for the whole evening and then tried to paw me on the way home.*

And then, once she thought of it, she was angry. No, she had been angry since the beginning of the party. Even before that. She had been angry ever since she'd rigged herself up in those ridiculous clothes. After that point nothing had pleased her. Surely there had been people to talk with at the party, or something she could have done to help, if she had really made an effort.

For that matter, now that she was taking a hard look at her own behavior, she could have gone to stand near Charlie instead of finding corners to hide in. Perhaps he would not have had so much to drink if she had been there, if she had relaxed and enjoyed what there was to enjoy.

No. For her there was little to enjoy there, and it was no

use pretending otherwise. What she should have done was go home and let Charlie have his "good time" without her. But that was the problem under it all. She wanted to have a good time, and she wanted to go out with Charlie. She hated the way he had acted the night before, and she found his drinking repulsive. She knew she was just one of the dozens of girls around him and that she should walk off and wash her hands of him while she still could do so without getting hurt. She knew that, but. . .

Charlie had something that drew her, even against her will. Some spark in his zest for life that caught her, even though she sensed a desperation under that zest.

What was it, she wondered, that drove him to such frantic play? Why was he bored one minute and rushing through life the next? How could he paw her and bruise her when he was the same gentle giant who had taught her to fly the dragon? She'd been nervous about his closeness that first day, and she was certain he knew it. He had been careful to let her know that he would not harm her, and she had gradually accepted his arms around her, had felt safe enough inside their circle to learn from him about the dragon.

He was a puzzle, a helter-skelter mixture of wonderful and terrible. She didn't understand him and didn't think she ever would. He was the adventurous hero one minute and the source of fear the next.

The one thing she knew was that he and she had nothing in common. Nothing. Whatever it was between them was finished before it started. She would be better off if she had nothing to do with him at all. Safer.

I wish I'd told him off, she thought. *I should have told him to keep his hands to himself and to. . .*

Next time I see him I'll..

She sighed. She was better off without him.

What she needed was somebody stable and solid, somebody she felt safe with, somebody she understood. Like Ewald Phipps. That's what her parents said. Often. Usually right after they reminded her that she wasn't getting any younger.

Mrs. Ewald Phipps. Mrs. Martha Phipps. She sighed again. *Not that, please not that.*

She would have to try harder to have this one summer of good times, just this one, before she gave up. But how? So far she was doing very badly indeed. About the best thing she had done was meet Charlie. And go on the whale watch. And meet the professor. Adam.

Adam was good looking. Even Bree thought so. And he was adventurous. Nobody else she knew spent days on boats and in helicopters searching the sea for whales. Certainly not Ewald. Ewald was a good man with a good job, a respected place in the community, and not one ounce of excitement. He was familiar, comfortable, dull.

Adam was comfortable too. He was quiet, like she was, and religious. She hadn't expected that. She'd grown up with serious Christians and was accustomed to them as a part of her life, so of course she was more comfortable with Adam. She hadn't expected to run into a Christian who acted like the other Christians she knew, not way out here, not in her new lifestyle. She wasn't sure she liked it. It bothered her. If Adam had been an atheist, she would have found that easier to deal with, almost. As it was, as long as Adam was there to remind her, she would have a harder time closing the doors to her old ways. She halfway resented him for reminding her of what she was at home. The other half of her reached toward the comfort he offered. With Adam, she didn't have to explain her background. He would understand why she didn't know how to be a good-time girl. He might even understand why she wanted to try. He just wouldn't approve.

She wondered what he would have said if he had seen her in the party get-up last night. She could imagine. It would be approximately what her father would have said. It would be close to what she herself would say, if someone asked her.

Adam would never see her like that because she would never look like that again. On Thursday, when she and Adam would go to the Pilgrim Monument, she would wear one of those print skirts and soft blouses that she felt comfortable in. She would dress the way she liked to dress, no matter what Bree said.

She would enjoy another afternoon with Adam. It would be a relief after being with Charlie. With Adam there was no romantic pretense, only friendship, possibly the beginnings of a very good friendship. She didn't have to try to be mysterious or amusing. She could just relax. They would talk and see new things and she would get to know this tall, lean, quiet man.

And she would forget about Charlie.

six

At one o'clock Thursday afternoon, two bells by ship's time, Muffie parked her car near Macmillan Pier in Provincetown and walked toward the end of the pier. She didn't get far before she saw Adam striding to meet her, extending his hand in greeting and looking glad to see her again.

She took his hand and smiled up at him.

"You came," he said.

"Of course. I said I would."

He acknowledged that with a nod and with the smallest of smiles. They stood there awkwardly for a moment, then he pulled her hand through his other arm, holding it there, and she did not pull away.

The walk to the monument was more like a hike than a stroll. Adam walked in the same manner he did everything else—purposefully. His step was long and his pace fast. He moved through the pedestrian and motor traffic in a direct line and nothing stayed in his path. Muffie wondered if others got out of his way because of his serious look or because he seemed unlikely to stop.

She was walking faster than she ever did by herself, trying not to lag behind, following the pull on her hand. She took a little running step to keep up.

He turned. "Too fast?"

"A little."

"Sorry. I'm not used to walking with anyone. There isn't

any hurry." He slowed down and she began to catch her breath. Once or twice Adam picked up speed without seeming to realize it, but the tug of her hand on his arm reminded him and he slowed down again.

He didn't talk. She didn't either, at first because she needed her breath for keeping up with him, and then because he seemed preoccupied. After that she kept her silence out of curiosity. She wondered what he would say, finally, and when.

Atop the highest hill in town, the obelisk monument rose needle-like toward the sky. Although the road approached it as gradually as possible, the walk was steep. The professor, however, climbed at the same speed he walked and she panted along behind, arriving quite out of breath. He didn't turn to look at her, not once.

At the entrance he paid their admission, and they pushed through the turnstile. He turned left and she followed. The museum was small, but the exhibits were interesting. She wandered along slowly, trying to take in each item. He moved ahead of her, sometimes finding himself too distant and returning to where she lagged behind, inspecting some antique tool or item of clothing.

While she studied the exhibits, he studied her. In the few quick glances she gave him, she caught a look compounded of surprise, a little impatience, and something else she couldn't identify—possibly a trace of reluctant admiration.

Adam only partly understood these things himself. He was an expert on whales, not on young ladies. He knew the feeding habits and behavioral characteristics, as much as they were known by anyone, of several varieties of cetaceans. He lived as closely with them as he could.

His recent experience with young ladies was both wider and more limited. He had met many more of this species than he had of the whales. Smiling lips and fluttering eyelashes were part of his daily milieu. He was aware that several of these ladies had tried to encourage his friendship, and he recognized that they seemed unaccountably taken by him. Indeed, he had overheard enough of their comments to know that some of their behavior was directly attributable in some way to the blueness of his eyes.

However, so far the young ladies had been remarkably similar. Quite a number of them belonged to the student-in-love-with-the-professor subspecies, a most annoying variety that tended to cluster in groups and giggle. They often hung around at the end of class to ask endless pointless questions about subjects they cared nothing about.

Another subspecies he knew well was the professional woman. These were easier for him to be with, since they had given up giggling and tended to be more sensible, more practical. One of these had almost become his wife, until she had become discouraged by his refusal to follow her aggressive plan for his career advancement.

Some of the women he had met fit a category he loosely labeled "available." These were pleasant company, agreeable, and eager to be whatever he wanted them to be. Since he wanted them to be themselves, not a mirror of his ideas, he found them empty.

To be fair to all these ladies, he would have admitted readily that he was not at all interested in romantic entanglements. If a woman was independent, she interfered with his work. If she was dependent on his moods, he found her hollow. If she adored him, he doubted her intelligence.

This one, with her quiet manner and slender grace, was

different. Her looks were more than satisfactory. She might even be called beautiful. Her hair was rich, with reddish glints in the warm brown, and her skin was a delicate peach that still, after several weeks on the cape, was almost as light as it had been when he'd first met her. And her eyes, with their sudden flash of green—she was most definitely beautiful.

She was serious. He liked that. The girl had depth and a lively mind. Her questions were thoughtful and seemed to spring from a genuine desire to know. There was so much he could teach her.

She was beginning to matter to him, and he didn't know if he liked that. If she stayed in his thoughts as she had the last week, she would interrupt his work, become a nuisance. The sensible thing to do would be to see her now and then but not get too involved.

She looked up at him just then and he caught the flash of green eyes. *Too late*, he thought, impatient at his own weakness. *Too late*.

He led her out to the grassy terrace surrounding the monument. In this area of sand and sparse grass, the putting-green perfection of the carefully tended grass was a striking setting. In its way, it was more impressive than were the beds of flowers around it.

"Grass," she said in a surprised voice, and he felt a race of satisfaction in her perception.

"It's difficult to grow grass like that here," he responded. "Too much salt."

She said, "I wondered what you'd say first." When he blinked, caught off balance by her comment, she went on. "You haven't spoken since the pier. I haven't either."

He said no more but led her to the monument itself and

into the base, then followed her up the tight winding stairs toward the top. She tried to climb quickly, knowing he would move quickly if alone, but she ran out of breath and stopped twice, briefly. Along the way she noticed that some of the stones of the outside wall were engraved with names of states or of organizations or of communities. On her second stop she asked about them.

"Gifts for the construction of the tower," he said. "They wanted to have a part in it. The blocks are granite and very expensive, particularly since there is no granite around here. It's the tallest all-granite monument in the United States."

From then on she read each block until at last she reached the open observation platform on the top. She looked out over the nearby houses and shops to the sea, which beckoned her as it always did. She inhaled deeply, smelling that indefinable sea smell.

"That's Long Point Light, that last one on the end of land curving around the harbor. Then Wood End Light to the right. We passed those on the way out to search for whales."

She nodded at his explanation. "Stahlwagon Banks are. . .?"

"Over there," he finished, pointing the opposite direction, and they walked around to look from the opposite side of the observation platform. "From here they are only water, indistinguishable from the rest of the sea, but when you get closer in the helicopter, they are a different color. The water is shallower, not so deep a blue."

They looked from each of the four sides, and he identified the sights she knew along with others she had never heard of. It all looked different from up here—older, quainter, and more sprawling than she had thought it was.

She wished she had brought her camera, but then she remembered she always took pictures and then afterward forgot to look at them. *I might just as well try to keep it in my memory with the rest of this summer*, she thought, and looked long and hard before turning to descend. On the way down she reread some of the stones, in case she had missed any. It was her nature to see it all, everything, instead of breezing past.

For lunch, he took her to a tiny restaurant with umbrella tables on a back deck overlooking the beach. She sat in the blue-and-white director's chair next to his.

"It's a lovely day," she said, looking out over the water.

"Yes," he said, seeing the way she leaned her determined little chin on her hand and following with his eyes the graceful line of her forearm. It was the same delicate peach as her cheek, except for a blue-black mark above the wrist. He reached out to touch it, to pull it toward him. She winced as his hand closed over the mark.

"What happened?" he said, inspecting the bruise.

"An accident," she said, not meeting his eyes.

He stroked it lightly with his finger and then carefully fitted his hand around her wrist and measured his grip against the bruise. "It looks like the mark of a hand, a very big hand."

She tried to withdraw her arm, but he held it gently out between them. The waiter appeared at that moment, and she pulled again at her arm. This time Adam released it.

They ordered and the waiter was gone before Adam asked again, "What happened?"

She shrugged.

He said, "How's Charlie?"

She tried to brush the question away. "There's nothing

between Charlie and me. There never was, really. I'll probably never see him again."

"You said that last time we met, just before he showed up on the beach looking for you. Did Charlie do this?"

"He didn't mean to," she said.

"What else did he do to you?" demanded Adam.

"Nothing." She saw the concern in his face and deliberately laughed lightly. "Don't worry about me. I can take care of myself."

He said, "I don't know about that."

She didn't know about that either, right at that moment, but she said no more on the matter. Instead she led him into a discussion of the preservation of whales and, by the time her lobster roll appeared, he seemed to have forgotten the bruise.

She hadn't, though. She listened to Adam, trying to concentrate, trying to put in an appropriate word here and there, but it was difficult to brush aside his concern. It was tempting to tell him the whole story, about how frightened she was and how helpless. What would he say to that? She decided against it.

Adam is a gentle man, she thought, *but this would make him angry. He would not placidly accept hurt to a friend. And he likes me. I can tell by the way he studies me when he thinks I'm not watching and by the way he anticipates my questions sometimes*. She smiled to herself and refocused on the wanton destruction of whales.

They lingered over lunch until time for supper. Then they wandered out to the end of the pier to watch for fishing boats coming in with their catches. There were no boats to watch, but it didn't matter.

"Are you hungry?" he asked, very much later.

"I should go," she answered.

At her car he said, "My church has a chowder supper every Tuesday night. Do you like chowder?"

"I don't know."

He said, "They also have corn on the cob."

She smiled. "I like corn."

So it was settled and they parted, he to walk back to his single room and she to drive back to Wellfleet.

It was a pleasant afternoon, all in all—a quiet one. When she was with Adam things seemed to settle down to a calm that she absorbed. With Charlie she was always on edge, off center, trying to say and do the right thing without making a fool of herself and then finding herself in difficulty. Each time was like that. Every single time she saw Charlie was a challenge that ended in a fight.

Okay, not a fight. A struggle, a shout, or a battle for her survival. Why couldn't he be gentle like Adam?

But Charlie was gentle, she thought, remembering the tentative way he had touched her cheek and his patience when they had flown the kite. He just. . .lost it sometimes. There was so much of him that he seemed almost unable to manage it all. He needs. . .

She didn't know what he needed. Control, for a start. And some maturity. Peace? Yes. Definitely, he needed peace. A solid shaking up of his thinking? "A good swift kick," she said aloud, and then she regretted it. He would get one of those someday. Somebody would see to it. Not her. She was too small, too insignificant to matter to him, but somebody would really hurt him. Then what?

Not that it mattered to her, of course. She wouldn't be seeing Charlie.

She didn't see him. She worked at the Salt Pond

Visitors' Center giving out information and he, apparently, stayed on the beach.

On Saturday she gave her shipwreck talk, her best one yet, and she loved it. She didn't think of Charlie at all then, except for one tiny part when she filled waiting hands with sand to make waves.

She volunteered to work Sunday, knowing that most of the crew would be recovering from the beach party Charlie had asked her to. Charlie didn't appear, but she kept too busy to notice. Almost.

She wouldn't think about him anymore. She had Tuesday to look forward to. Charlie never crossed her mind at all, except that now and then she saw the bruise. It was lighter now and would soon disappear and then she could forget Charlie entirely.

Tuesday after work she showered and dressed carefully, wearing the lavender dress she had waited so long to find an occasion for. Bree watched without comment until she was giving a last brush through her hair.

"You look nice," Bree conceded.

Muffie said, "I thought you didn't like this dress."

"I was wrong," said Bree. "Evidently I was wrong about the professor, too. You don't think he's dull at all, do you."

It wasn't a question, so Muffie didn't answer it except to smile. Her relationship with Bree had changed after that party, had lost its easy openness. Since then they were careful what they said to each other. Neither wished to bring unspoken irritation into the open for fear of causing a rift they could not heal.

"Aren't you going to ask about Charlie?" Bree ventured.

"No."

Bree said, "He asks about you."

Muffie pretended serious interest in a wayward curl. She asked, very casually, "What do you tell him?"

Bree said, "What do you want me to tell him?"

"Nothing," said Muffie. "Tell him nothing." She flipped her curl one last time, picked up her little matching jacket and her purse, nodded a good-bye, and went out and downstairs to wait outside, away from Bree and her questions.

She didn't have long to wait. Adam was as punctual as the town clock, driving up in his battered gray pickup just as she heard the seven bells for seven-thirty. Six bells for seven o'clock, she counted, and one more for the half hour.

His car was like his clothes, she thought: good quality, serviceable, clean, and full of wrinkles and holes. It was unimportant as a status symbol, but essential to maintaining his everyday life.

He was dressed up tonight. He had exchanged his usual garb for gray trousers and a light blue shirt, both fairly wrinkle-free, and his shoes had evidently had a recent near-miss with the polish. His hair was shower damp and still looked combed in back, although the front had begun to go its own way.

Amused by his efforts, and flattered, Muffie wondered why she had fussed over each curl and smoothed each wrinkle in her dress. She might as well have tumbled downstairs in something from the unpressed pile Bree was accumulating in her corner again. Adam would never notice.

But he did notice and was impressed. He said so and his expression confirmed it. She imagined that he stood a bit straighter next to her and walked more jauntily than usual. As he drove, his eyes lingered on her more than they should have if he wanted to see where he was going. She found herself keeping watch on the road for him, in case he forgot.

"It's green," she pointed out when they had sat through most of their turn at the light. "Watch that red car," she said at one point, and "You're over the line, I think." He was over the line at least four feet.

"Sorry," she said. "You don't need me to tell you how to drive."

He smiled into her eyes and went through a stop sign.

"Yes, you do," she said. "Slow down!"

She was thoroughly nervous by the time they parked behind the church. "Do you always drive like that?" she wanted to know.

"Like what?"

She didn't answer. At least she knew now why his car was battered. It had probably gotten crunched in the first week of his ownership. If that's what happened to his car, she wondered what had made his clothes go to pieces. That man needed a keeper—someone to sew his buttons on and keep him from getting killed in traffic.

Considering his interest in food (minimal) and his manner of getting to it, she was afraid to speculate on the quality of the chowder dinner. It was probably one of those potluck dinners where it was better not to know who cooked it. She decided to try to ignore, as much as she could, any foreign objects floating in her soup and any unknown substance glued to her spoon. She braced herself and entered the fellowship hall.

A recent addition, it was built onto the back of the church and shared, at the opposite end, a corridor with the main part of the church. The original section was traditional Cape in style and the new part was a modern variation on the same theme. One whole side of glass and greenery gave an open, airy feeling to the interior, a melding of inside with outside.

Everyone knew Adam and wanted to know Muffie. They greeted her warmly, extended their obvious friendship for him to her, and made room for Adam and Muffie at the long table in the center of the hall.

Muffie tried so hard not to notice dirt that she actually hunted for it so she could overlook it. There wasn't any. The serving table and what she could see of the kitchen through the pass-through window were spotless, as clean as her mother's own kitchen.

The food smelled good. She sniffed it as unobtrusively as possible as she carried her tray to the table and sat down. After the prayer she took a good look at her dinner. The corn looked perfect and the hot biscuit was tempting. The chowder—it was clam chowder. Those gray-brown lumps lurking about near the top of the hot milky liquid had to be clams.

She stirred and watched the lumps circle. They bore little resemblance to the raw clam she had somehow downed in P'town, but the memory was difficult to push aside. She looked at the chowder and saw raw clam on the half shell.

A furtive glance at Adam told her he was involved in active conversation with the older man across the table. She pushed the chowder to one side and ate the corn. The biscuit went in a few bites. The chowder remained.

She stirred it again and watched the lumps float. She took a spoonful and raised it to her mouth. She put the spoonful back in the bowl and the spoon on the tray and turned to the lady next to her to seek diversion in conversation.

Did she like the new fellowship hall? Was she here for a

visit? Mrs. Beale was easy to talk to and reminded Muffie of people in her home church. The conversation moved from general to specific without being uncomfortably prying. Even a tentative query about her relationship to Adam was gently phrased and easily answered: "Friends, just friends."

Another lady across the table entered the conversation and then introduced the young couple next to her, and Muffie felt on friendly terms with a tableful of people. It was fun, like the carry-in suppers in the church basement at home. She hadn't realized how much she missed them.

Of course, the food at home was better. She didn't have gray-brown lumps of dead clam to contend with. One good thing about Indiana was the almost total absence of clams. She looked down at her bowl with regret, wishing she could pay her host church the compliment of eating what they offered.

Her bowl was empty. Except for her biscuit, there was no food on her tray.

Biscuit?

She looked at Adam. He was still involved in conversation with the man across from him and still finishing his chowder. Her chowder? She stared at him suspiciously. He felt it and looked directly at her with no change of expression at all, none that she could see.

He said, "If you'd like more chowder, help yourself."

She was almost sure she saw a trace of a smile as he turned away.

Mrs. Beale was watching, twinkling with secret knowledge.

Muffie said, "Did Adam. . .?"

Mrs. Beale nodded and laughed, then passed the butter

for Muffie's second biscuit.

Later, in the car, he said, "Would you like to get a bite to eat? You didn't have much supper."

"I wasn't very hungry," she said.

"Clams?"

"Clams," she agreed, and allowed herself to shudder. "Sorry. I could have eaten them if I had tried harder. I think. Charlie says. . ."

"Charlie? Are we talking about the same Charlie who bruised your arm?"

"Yes, but—"

"I know," said Adam, "he didn't mean to do it and besides, you don't see him any more."

"That's right," she said.

"I hope so," said Adam.

"Red light," said Muffie. "How do you drive when I'm not with you?"

He said, "It's easier. I concentrate on the road."

"Concentrate," she said. "We can talk later."

He did, and she didn't have to warn him about his driving again, not once, all the way to the ice cream stand.

"Stay in the car," he ordered.

She stayed. At last he returned, bearing two enormous ice cream cones. "Coconut almond or cranberry?"

She took the cranberry.

"Now," he said, "we talk. You are going to tell me who you really are and what you want."

"I've already told you who I am."

He said, "Yes, a girl from Indiana who is spending the summer lecturing about shipwrecks and listening to my lectures on whales."

"Right."

"That's not enough. There are too many gaps. First of all, you're a teacher, but you never mention your students. You're the only teacher I've ever met that doesn't mention her work. Why? And why do you try so hard to fit in with Bree and her crowd? And what's with you and Charlie? What are you going to do when—"

"I don't have to answer all these questions," she said.

He said, "But I wish you would."

"Why?"

"Because it's important to me. You're important to me."

"Then let me alone," she snapped. His deep blue eyes widened, but his gaze was steady. Hers faltered and shifted away. "I'm sorry," she said.

"Tell me."

"There's nothing to tell."

"All right," he said at last. "I suppose I have to accept that, for now. But I'd feel better about it if I thought you really knew what you are doing."

"That's what my father said," said Muffie. "Let's talk about something else."

"Not whales," he said.

They talked about the chowder supper and the new addition and the people she had met. He told her about the Sunday school class he taught and about his concern for the young people of the church. He would be here only a year and most of that was gone. His sabbatical ended with the beginning of the fall term and after that he would be back only for summers to continue his research. The church here was important to him in offering him a spiritual home away from his own home and in offering a place to be of service. He would miss it when he left.

She mentioned that she missed her church. Sundays didn't

feel like Sundays without it. She told him how she had thought about going to church in Wellfleet, and how the bells on Sunday reminded her each week. "I almost went last Sunday, but—"

"Come with me next Sunday," he said. "You already know some of the people and you know me. You can even drive, if you feel safer."

She laughed. "It's a date."

He drove her home, concentrating. She listened to the rattles of the car and tried not to think about his driving. They parked in front of her apartment. He killed the engine and the rattles, and they could hear the night sounds of the quiet neighborhood.

She heard the bird first, her bird, and called his attention to it. "What is it?" she asked.

Adam listened. "A mockingbird, close by."

"He must be very beautiful," she said.

"He looks like a thinnish robin," said Adam, "but gray with white patches on his wings and tail. To look at him you'd never suspect him of cleverly mimicking the songs of the other birds, but that's what he does. In fact, it's his name—Mimus polyglottos—many-tongued mimic."

"What does his own song sound like?"

"He doesn't usually sing his own song, not like most other birds, although sometimes he seems to sing something original. Mostly he copies other birds, or music on the radio, or even a passing cat. He's so good at it that people tend to forget which part of his song is his own. They recognize him by the way he tries to sound like the others, although he never quite matches exactly. He is also loud, as you notice, and he sings at any odd hour. It's like he's determined to be noticed even if he has to be somebody he isn't."

"That's rather sad, isn't it?" Muffie asked.

"I don't imagine he thinks so. No more than you think it's sad when you—"

"When I what?" asked Muffie.

"Never mind. Forget I said it." Adam reached for her hand and held it in his own, inspecting it, weighing it, memorizing it. "Muffie, I—"

He felt her hand stiffen and saw she was watching the open four-wheel drive that was just parking across the street. Adam recognized them all but the dark-haired girl in the back seat with Charlie. They all were watching, but neither he nor Muffie greeted them as he got out and opened the door for Muffie. He walked her up the stairs and at the door Adam said, "I'd like to kiss you, but I won't."

"Thank you," she said, and went in, leaving Adam standing there listening to the song of the mockingbird.

seven

"Bree, we've got to talk," said Muffie over the morning tea and blueberry muffin.

Bree looked pained. "Not you too," she said. "Don't tell me. You want me to settle down and be serious, right? That's all I hear from Jack and now you're starting in on me too. Forget it. I can put up with your stuffy attitude until September. I can tolerate your compulsion for neatness. I can even overlook your disapproval of me and my friends. But I am not going to listen to you tell me how to live. Forget it."

"That's not what I want to say at all," said Muffie. "All I meant was that you and I have been distant from each other since the night we went to the party and that I wanted to see if we could get back to the way we were. This chilly truce is hard to live with."

"You started it," Bree charged. "You with your snobby attitude. You go to a party and spend the whole time looking down on all of us. Then you act like you never saw anybody with a little too much to drink, like it was all beneath you or something. How do you think I feel? How would you feel?"

"Angry, I guess," said Muffie.

"Right."

Muffie nodded. "I don't blame you. I'm sorry. The truth is that before the party, I really never did see anyone with too much to drink—not up close. I didn't know how to

115

handle it—I still don't. I wasn't looking down on you, at least I don't think I was. I was just confused and lost. I felt like I didn't belong there, and I probably didn't. Those things are not fun to me. I felt safer on the sidelines."

"I thought you wanted to be the original good-time girl," gibed Bree. "You can't even survive one party. You don't know what you want."

"I guess that's about it," Muffie said. "I know you tried to help, and I appreciate it, even if it didn't work out. I just don't think I'm the party type. I don't like the drinking, and I don't like what happens to people when they drink too much."

"Are you trying to say I shouldn't drink?" Bree sounded angry again.

"I think you wouldn't if you could see what it does to you."

"Jack always tells me I should quit, too, but he doesn't really mind."

"Are you sure? Did you ask him?" Muffie asked. "If he really loves you, he would want you safe. I want you safe, and I'm only your friend, not the man who loves you." Muffie knew from the look on Bree's face that she had said more than Bree wanted to hear. "Please try to understand," she said. "I don't mean to tell you what to do. It's only that I'm not comfortable with these things. I tried to explain that to Charlie, but it made him angry."

"It sure did. Charlie's still angry. What did you do to him, anyway?"

"I told him no."

"Everybody says no, but nobody means it," said Bree.

"I meant it," said Muffie.

She told Bree about the last conversation she'd had with

Charlie, the one where he'd walked off angry, and then she had to explain about the struggle in the back seat, which Bree knew about because she had been there. Bree seemed to think Muffie was being prissy.

Muffie showed Bree the blue mark around her wrist. "I have a couple of other bruises that don't show, places that caught the wrong side of his elbow or something. I'm not sure exactly how I got them. I was too scared to think about anything but getting out of that car."

Bree inspected the mark. She said slowly, "Charlie would never do this. He couldn't. He doesn't have a mean thought. I know him. There must be some mistake."

"My mistake," said Muffie. "I shouldn't have been there, and I really don't think Charlie knew what he was doing. Charlie scares me, especially when he drinks."

"You'd rather go out with Professor Dull."

"Adam doesn't get drunk, and he doesn't hurt me. And he's not dull. You wouldn't say he was dull if you ever saw the way he drives." Muffie laughed and explained about Adam's driving and soon the two were laughing together almost as easily as they had at the beginning of the summer.

In no time they were laughing about the raw clam and Bree's piles of clothing and were filling each other in on the latest news about the professor and Charlie and Jack.

Jack wasn't so much fun anymore, not to Bree. He was too serious, she said. He was getting annoying about it, complaining that party life was tiresome and that he wanted to quit playing games. He was pressing her to marry him, to settle down, raise a family. She'd been putting him off since last summer, but it was getting more difficult. One of these days she'd have to give a definite answer and she didn't want to.

"I need more time," she said. "I'm not ready for marriage. I can't take the serious stuff."

"Being serious has its advantages," suggested Muffie.

"For you, maybe," was Bree's answer. "If Jack would forget this nonsense about marriage, we could relax and have a good time. I'd like just once to go through a whole week without explaining why I can't accept that diamond ring he carries around in his pocket. I ought to just take it and then he'll be satisfied."

Muffie said, "Not for long. He would expect you to marry him and he might not be willing to wait ten years for the wedding. Do you love Jack?"

"Probably. Who knows? I'd hate to lose him; he can be a lot of fun. But. . ." Bree shrugged. "I just know I'm not going to do what my mother did—fall in love and get married to someone who leaves me and my kid when times get tough. All Mom ever did was work. Not me. I'm going to make my good times last as long as I can."

Now that she and Bree were friendly again, Muffie felt better, although she was sure the conversation had changed nothing. Maybe she should have kept her mouth shut about the drinking, but it really wasn't good for Bree and—

Martha was at it again, putting her nose in everybody's business, taking care of people, trying to make things work out right. Just when she thought she was getting the feeling of being a Muffie, she was back to being a Martha, worrying about people who were important to her. *That's what's wrong with me*, she thought. *I always worry about other people, making them and their worries the center of my life. I'm not that important to them*.

But Adam thought she was important. He had said so

and he wouldn't say it lightly. He wouldn't do anything lightly. She tried to imagine him at play, hitting a baseball perhaps. She could picture that. He would concentrate on the weight of the bat and the speed of the ball, compute the physics involved, and hit at the angle and speed he calculated would send the ball in the direction he had judged to be most effective.

She smiled at her own exaggeration, recognizing the grain of truth in it. Adam was serious and solid, not like Charlie.

What difference did it make what Charlie was like? *Forget him*, she told herself. She had already begun, hadn't she? She had mentioned him only in passing in her letters home—those long, general letters she wrote once a week. How could she explain him? Instead she wrote of Bree and Jack and of Adam. She wrote about her job and about the shipwreck presentation, which was the best part of the job. Too bad it was only forty-five minutes long and only once a week. In winter she could spend her whole day teaching.

The part she liked best about her job here was the part she had done at home for years. She had come here to be different, or at least to begin being different, to forget who she was in the rest of her life and begin again. She had rarely been cornered the way Adam had cornered her with his persistent questions. He would ask again and what would she tell him? That she was in disguise as a Muffie? She hadn't even mentioned that part to her parents.

She never phoned home, but hid from their questions in letters. Their letters to her were warm and loving, with no criticism. They asked about her job, her friends, her health, but they never asked if she was living the exciting new life she had come there for. They always ended the same way, with a promise to keep her in their prayers.

At night she lay awake listening to her bird with his counterfeit songs, wondering which part of the melody was his own. Poor bird. He had lost his own song, his own identity. *Like me*, she thought. *Whose song do I sing? Am I a sober, serious, intellectual match for a sober, serious professor, or am I a good-time girl who hasn't figured out how to have the good times?*

I'm all of those and none, she decided. *I'm a teacher who loves to teach but wants more in her life than just teaching. I'm a daughter who wants the love of her parents without being the person they know. I want the laughs, but I want them with serious people. I found the party depressing and empty, but how full am I?*

If I'm not careful, she realized, *I will lose myself in this muddle. I'll try so many ways of being that I won't know who or what I am. Just like the mockingbird.*

She heard Jack's car drive up and looked out to see only Jack and Bree in it. Concluding that Charlie must be out with Anita, Muffie went to sleep thinking about that.

In the morning Bree was nervous and snappy and didn't want to talk. The ride to work was unnaturally quiet. Muffie opened the conversation several times, but Bree let it die. After a while Muffie quit trying, deciding that something must have happened with Jack, but Bree wasn't ready to talk about it.

Fridays were busy days at the center. Most tourists came and went on Saturday, so the lobby was full of people leaving the next day who wanted to squeeze in one last attraction or buy one more poster before they had to leave their vacations behind. A few of the people, the paler ones, were newcomers who asked the usual questions about what the center offered. By closing time she was exhausted and ready for a can of soup and a hot shower. She was not ready for Charlie.

He was leaning against her car door when she came out. He lounged there, dwarfing the car and looking almost plastic in his perfect tan and perfect muscles. He didn't move when she approached with the key in her hand.

"Excuse me," she said, holding the key out and waiting for him to move away from the lock.

He didn't move except to grasp the extended arm firmly but very gently and lift it to inspect her wrist. It was perfectly all right. "The other one," he said, and then raised that wrist for inspection. She winced but said nothing, hoping he had not seen, but he had. He fitted his hand over the mark, circling her delicate arm with his fingers and looking to see that the marks on her arm did indeed match the placing of his fingers.

"I did this," he said, stroking the bruise lightly, very lightly with the back of his hand.

"Yes."

"I didn't know till Bree told me. I'm sorry."

She said, "It's all right."

"It's not all right. I don't know what happened. I would never—I mean—Bree said you had some other bruises."

"They'll go away," she said. "It wasn't the bruises as much as the way you were that night. You—"

"I scared you. Bree told me."

She looked up at him and into his eyes. "You just wouldn't stop," she said, "and I tried to tell you no but you wouldn't listen. I tried to stop you but it was. . .very difficult."

"I'm sorry." He looked sorry. His eyes were softer and sadder than she had ever seen them, softer than she had imagined they could be. His laughter was gone for a change, and he looked down at her with his plea for forgiveness written across his face.

She said, "I know you didn't mean it. I'm just not used to the way you do things. Where I come from, no means no, and I've never had to fight to keep it that way. I've also never been out with anyone who was drunk. I didn't like that part either."

"You'd better get used to it if you're going to get along in the world," he said.

She thought it over and said, "I don't think so. I think I can get along without that. I don't like what it does to people. I don't like what it does to you. If that's what I have to do to get along in the world, then maybe I won't get along. Maybe the world will have to go on its way without me."

He regarded her thoughtfully. "You really mean that, don't you. You're ready to take on the whole world."

"No," she said, "I'm not ready for that, but I will stand my ground if I have to."

"Even if you get bruised?"

"Even then," she answered.

They studied each other for a moment. She saw a giant of a man quieted by his own guilt and made serious by his effort to understand. He looked so forlorn that she only narrowly resisted the impulse to reach out to him with a comforting hand on his arm. Her hand paused in midair between them.

He reached out as if he wanted to pull her into his arms, but stopped.

They spoke together. "It's all right," she said, and "I'm sorry," he said. In different circumstances it would have made them smile, but not now. She merely nodded and looked steadily into his sad brown eyes as he went on.

"I'll never hurt you again," he said, "and neither will anyone else. Not if I can help it. I swear it."

"Don't swear."

"But I promise—"

"Don't. You can't be sure what you'll do next time you drink too much. What good is a promise you can't keep?"

"It's a promise all the same, whether you accept it or not," he said.

"As long as you drink, there's only one way to keep that promise," she said. "Stay away from me. Far away, so that I don't begin to trust you too much again."

"That's unreasonable," he objected. "I can understand that you're cautious about trusting me, but we can still—"

"No," she said, watching the softness in his face give way to frustration.

"Okay," he said. "Have it the way you want it. You go hide in your own little corner and let life go by without you." His volume increased with his frustration level. "Not me. Not Charlie. I've got a lot of living to do yet and a lot of parties to go to, and a lot of girls to take to those parties. There's no use wasting my time and sympathy on a girl who's too dumb to know what she really wants." He straightened, glared once at her, then marched off.

"Have a good time," she called.

"I intend to," he shouted, not turning around.

"Good-bye," she said firmly, but he could not have heard. "Good-bye," she whispered, and swallowed, holding back tears. "So much for the party girl," she said to herself in the car. Her head ached with the effort of not crying. Her body ached from the day at work. And her spirit ached from. . .she didn't know what her spirit ached from.

She stopped at the gas station to telephone Adam. No, she couldn't go out with him tonight. No, not church either. Nor lunch after church. Thanks anyway. Maybe another time, maybe when she felt better. Sorry.

By the time she stretched out on her own bed, still in her work clothes, she knew she didn't really want to feel better. Not then. Not if it took any effort. She just wanted to lie there and sink into the mattress and rest.

Bree didn't come home for supper. The radio was too much bother to turn on. Supper didn't sound good. Through closed windows, voices came and went on the street below, but none interested her. She simply lay there, absolutely still, until she dozed off.

She awoke to stifling heat and darkness. She looked at her watch. Almost eleven. Bree would be home in two or three hours. Until then, there was no one around but that bird, that loud-mouthed mockingbird with everybody's song but his own. Even with the window shut she could hear him. If she opened the window to let fresh air in, the song would be inescapable. She felt trapped.

She rose and left the apartment, driving through the cool darkness to the harbor. She parked near the end of the lot nearest the boats and sat listening to the night sounds of water slipping and slurping about the piling, boats nudging each other gently in the dark, teenagers at the ice cream stand at the far opposite end of the lot.

She listened sharply. *No mockingbird. Fine. Just fine.*

She slid down in the front seat so that her nose was just at windowsill level. She took a deep breath of the sea air and tried to make herself relax. *My car is like a capsule*, she thought, *and I'm closed neatly inside it like an animal invisible in his burrow, seeing but not being seen.* She liked that. It had a separate, unreachable feel to it that she found comforting. She needed to be separate for a while so she could think, could center in on important things, the truth. Alone, she could feel closer to God.

And there she was, at the heart of it.

She sighed.

In the harbor the small boats bobbed gently against the piling. Far out a tiny light shone from a moving boat. *He's a long way out,* she thought. *I wonder if he feels lost out there. Like me. He must know the way home. When he's done he'll go home again and tie up, another little boat safe in the harbor. And me?*

I don't even know which direction to head in. I want too many things that don't go together. I want fun and friends and. . .too many things.

Should I pray for all these things I want? Would God listen to such a selfish prayer?

Of course He'll listen, but that doesn't mean He'll give me what I ask for. Besides, He already knows what I want, even if I don't.

What do I want? "Please, God, help me know what I want," she prayed.

The little boats bobbed gently on the water and the tiny light stayed tiny. She listened to the night noises and thought. There were no answers.

Well, I can at least make peace with Charlie. Poor Charlie. Why "poor"? Because he's so unhappy. He scares me, but I think he scares himself more. If I'd spent more time listening to him and less time worrying about my-self, I'd have realized that sooner. There must be some way I can help him. If only. . .

She sat up straight and started the car. With a little luck

she might get back in time to catch Jack so he could help her find Charlie.

When she reached the apartment, Jack's car was parked out front. She parked and went up to Bree's side. "Hi," she said before she saw the huge person slouched down in the back seat.

"Hi," said all three, and then there was silence.

She took a deep breath and said, "Charlie, could we talk?"

"Sure. Talk."

"In private?" she said.

"Are you sure it's safe?" he asked.

"No," she said, "but I'll risk it."

"She'll risk it," Charlie told the others. "She'll risk talking with big bad Charlie." He didn't move.

She bristled and snapped back, "Forget it, Charlie. I thought we might be able to talk, but it was a dumb idea. Forget it."

"Feisty," said Charlie, with a touch of admiration, and hauled himself up and out of the car. "Let's walk." He led off toward the harbor in the direction she had just come.

For a while they only walked, she hurrying to keep up with his long, easy strides. At the center of town he stopped and faced her.

"Well?" he demanded.

She began walking again, more slowly, letting him match his steps to hers. At the bottom of the main street she said, "I'm sorry, Charlie. I should have accepted your apology the way you meant it instead of—I'm sorry."

"You accepted my apology," he said. "It's me you don't want."

"That's not true, Charlie. I don't want to be angry with you for something you have no control over, and you know you have no control when you drink. I know you wouldn't hurt me on purpose, but. . ."

"But?" he prompted.

She didn't answer. Instead she said, "You're right about me hiding in my own little corner."

"I shouldn't have said that," he said. "I was angry."

"You were also right," she said. "And right about my not knowing what I want, too. I mean, I know I want to have a good time and all that, but when it comes down to the real thing, I back off. It doesn't make sense."

"It does to me," said Charlie. "You're just out there playing in the wrong game, that's all. You don't even know the rules. No wonder you come out on the losing side."

"So teach me the rules, Charlie."

"No," he said. "Let's play a different game."

"I don't understand," she said.

As they made their way up and down the shadowy streets of the little village, he explained. He had done some thinking too, he said, and had decided he could not take the chance of hurting anyone because he lost control of himself. He was done with that. He had meant it when he'd said he would never hurt her again, and he intended to keep his promise whether she accepted his word or not. If that meant he had to give up drinking, then he would give it up. "I can and will give up drinking, if that's what it takes. In fact, I already have. I haven't touched a drop since the last time I talked to you."

"Why did you drink?"

"To shut off my thoughts," he said. "If I think, I'll remember that I'm only a small-time coach in a small-time high school instead of a power running back on a pro football team. I'll remember what my father wanted me to be and what a disappointment I am to him. I'm not a star, not a big name bringing big business to his firm, not even a little partner. Just a coach."

"Are you a good coach?"

He considered. "Yeah. Yeah, I guess I am."

"Do you like coaching?"

"Yeah. You should see those kids. They're quite a team. Last year we almost—yeah, I like it. I like it a lot."

"That's important, Charlie. You matter to all those kids, and you are happy being there. Why do you need to be something else?"

"Because," he said.

"No," she said. "In a few years those pro players will get hurt or old and have to quit. Then they'll have to find something else to do. If they're truly blessed, it will be something worth doing. You're already there, ahead of them, doing it. You're a winner the way you are, Charlie."

"You think so?" he asked. He stopped her and turned to read her eyes. "Am I a winner?"

"Absolutely," she said.

They walked on. After a while she wondered aloud if he would be able to get along without drinking. "I can," he said. "I will, although I would do better if you were with me. Would you go to the beach party with me tomorrow? It'll be a tamer party, and I won't make you ashamed of me, or afraid of me. I promise," he said. "Deal?"

"Deal," she said, and they shook on it. He kept her hand tucked inside his own as they walked on in silence, past the library and the church, past the shop on the corner, and up the silent street to her apartment.

At her stairs she said, on impulse, "Do you ever go to church, Charlie?"

He laughed. "If you've got any ideas about dragging me to church with you, now is the time to give them up. You've already made me give up my beer. If word ever gets out that I've done that for a girl, I'll never live it down. Don't make it any worse."

"I wasn't going to," she said. "I'm trying to make it better."

He took her hand, still enveloped in his own, and held it up to his eyes in the dim light. He rubbed a tentative thumb over the place where he thought the bruises were. She winced. He looked at her solemnly, and she saw the sadness in his eyes. He bent lightly to kiss the damaged wrist and then let her go, holding her only with his steady gaze.

She smiled slightly, in understanding, and turned without another word and went upstairs.

eight

Muffie worked the next day, Saturday, glad to have something on her mind besides the beach party. She was going for Charlie's sake, but she wasn't looking forward to it. Until she *had* to think about the party, she would think about what she was doing at work. On Saturdays, she always did her shipwreck talk.

She showed her map, demonstrated the abrasive action of the waves, showed photos of recent storm damage. The crowd, larger than usual, responded enthusiastically. They were absorbed in the presentation, and so was she.

Here is where I belong, she thought. *Whatever else I am or want, I am a teacher, a good one.*

"Your talk was very effective," said a quiet baritone voice near her. It so closely echoed her thoughts that she wondered if she had spoken them aloud.

She turned to find Adam smiling at her from the doorway, and she answered with a welcoming smile of her own. "Thank you, Adam. I love to teach."

"I can see that," he said. "How's the headache?"

"Better," she said.

"Good enough for church tomorrow?"

"No," she said. "I mean, I don't know. I mean. . .it's hard to explain."

"Care to try?" he said.

She shrugged and looked away, toward the sea. He lifted her knapsack with one hand and put the other arm around her shoulder. She stiffened and then gradually relaxed enough to lean trustingly against him for a moment, long enough for him to sniff her clean smell of soap and to feel a kind of astonished pleasure at having her close, long enough for him to want to keep her there. Too soon she stood away from him again, leaving an empty place near his heart.

Easy, Adam, he thought, catching his breath.

She stepped away from him, to the opposite side of the hut, and stood gazing at the sea. He crossed to that side, not too near her, and put the knapsack down on the bench against the wall. Then casually, as if the earth had not just quaked beneath him, he swung himself up onto the low wall. He sat facing the sea, legs swinging over the sand dune. Next to him he heard her sandy shoes scrunch on the cement floor, heard her hesitate, then heard her climb onto the bench and the shelf to sit next to him, not touching him.

After a little silence, he turned enough to lean his back against the corner, enough to see her. She flicked a glance at him, saw that he was watching, and looked away.

"I'm a good listener," he said. "A good teacher has to be a good listener. You know that."

She nodded. He waited. At last she said, "I did have a headache, but that's not the reason I don't want to go to church with you. I can't go. I. . ."

He waited.

She said, "I don't want to go. If I go to church and start my ordinary life all over again, I might as well go home. All my life I've gone to church, been well-behaved, done what I was supposed to do. I'm so used to doing what other people want that I don't even know what I want or who I really am. I'm not a real person. I'm just whatever I'm supposed to be, just dull old reliable M—" She stopped, closing her lips on the name.

He said nothing.

She sighed. "I want something else, something more."

"What do you want?"

"I don't know," she admitted in a very small voice. "I don't know. I asked God to help me know, but He didn't."

"When did you ask?"

"Yesterday," she said and then smiled ruefully. "That isn't much time to wait for His answer, is it? I guess I'd better wait a little longer. Only, what if I never find out? What if He answers and I don't understand the answer? What if I don't even hear it?"

"Are you listening?" asked Adam. "Are you opening your heart to Him and really listening?"

"I don't know," she answered. "Things keep getting in the way. I keep getting involved with people and losing my focus. First there's Bree and the way she is afraid to settle down. Then there's Charlie."

He answered carefully, "I thought that was over."

"It was," she said. "But he's so unhappy."

"I know."

"You do? Then you understand why that bothers me. He's too good to waste, too beautiful to destroy himself. How can I not try to help him?" She was almost pleading with him.

"And what about yourself?" Adam asked.

"I don't know," she said forlornly, holding back her tears.

He slid his hand across her shoulders, pulling her to lean against him, and she came into his arms. He circled them around her, protecting her, and she turned her face into his shoulder, tears finally spilling freely, silently.

"I'm sorry," she said, when the tears had nearly ended.

He wiped away the last of her tears very gently with his soft sleeve and touched her face where they had been. "Don't be," he said, holding her.

They talked long after that. She told him about the horrible party and how ashamed she was, and about how she wanted to be like Bree, except that she didn't really want to be like Bree, and about the way she wanted to have fun and was finding nothing really fun. Mostly he listened.

Suddenly it was late and she realized she had to go get ready for the beach party.

Reluctantly, he released her. She hopped down.

"Thanks," she said. "Thanks for being my friend."

He winced, then said, almost ruefully, "I really am your friend, you know. Remember that. You might need a friend some time."

She nodded and touched his arm in acceptance.

"Church tomorrow," he ordered. "I'll pick you up at nine. Be ready."

She hesitated, then shook her head. She raised one hand in farewell and ran off toward the parking lot, leaving him sitting alone on the wall.

By the time Charlie and Jack got to the apartment, she and Bree were ready in warm clothes, carrying jackets. Bree was edgy, restless, unhappy. Concerned, Muffie asked her what was wrong.

"What's wrong?" she answered. "You know what's wrong. Jack is wrong. All he talks about is getting married. I don't want to get married. He says I love him, but I don't want to. What good is love? People stop loving when they marry, so love doesn't count."

"It counts," said Muffie. "For some people it counts all their lives. You just have to work at it. At least that's what my parents say, and they ought to know. They've been married almost thirty-five years, and they still love each other."

"Imagine!" said Bree. "Thirty-five years. I wish—oh, there's Jack and Charlie." They snatched up their jackets and hurried out the door.

The crowd on the beach gathered in early dusk. The group laughed and played, running and rough-housing on the sand. A glow-in-the-dark Frisbee sailed back and forth until the darkness grew too deep. The die-hards, like Charlie, gave up the games then and joined in roasting hot dogs and toasting marshmallows at the huge bonfire. Chips and watermelon, washed down with cold drinks, completed the menu. Some of those cold drinks may have been beer, but Muffie didn't have any and neither did Charlie. When the heavy fog rolled in from the water, the air was heavy and wet and Muffie was glad to have her warm jacket and cap. The crowd settled into relative quiet around the fire. Charlie sprawled on the sand and pulled Muffie down to sit next to him in the glow of the fire. Somebody started a camp song and then another and another.

Muffie shivered and Charlie wrapped a heavy arm around her and pulled her inside his jacket. She welcomed the warmth, but she was wary, ready for another defensive fight against this huge, aggressive man.

"Relax," he whispered. "I won't hurt you."

She wriggled free, but when she found that he'd made no move to prevent her going, she settled back into the warmth of his jacket and gradually relaxed. He seemed less threatening than he had before. She didn't know how carefully he wrapped her, how aware he was of her beginnings of trust in him. She only knew that this Charlie was the Charlie who'd taught her to fly the dragon, and she was grateful to have him back.

The fog lifted, leaving a clear sky with a huge moon. The night was quiet now, except for subdued conversation and the steady rush of the waves. The beach at night was magic, a memory to keep, she thought, snuggling in silence next to the great warmth that was Charlie.

She studied him in the moonlight and found him magnificent. He turned to her and smiled, ruffled her curls with his free hand, and looked back toward the flames. They were content to sit in silence, listening to the sea and the crackling of the fire.

Jack and Bree were among the first to rise, and the four went home, still speaking in hushed tones. In the car Charlie took his usual two-thirds of the back seat, but he came no closer. Except for his arm on the back of her seat and his hand ruffling her hair, he made no attempt to be familiar. She yawned contentedly and he grinned.

At the apartment he suggested, "Let's walk," and they did, for half an hour, saying little, thinking much. At her stairs again, she said, "Thank you. It was beautiful."

"Yes," he said, and bent to kiss her lightly on the forehead. He ruffled her hair once more and was gone.

From her window in the dark apartment she could see him in the back seat, patiently waiting for Jack and Bree. *Charlie*, she thought, *beautiful Charlie*, and smiled to herself. *It was a lovely night.*

The glow from the beach bonfire lasted well into the next week. She discovered, when he came for her Sunday evening, that he had his own car. For no good reason, she had never given it a thought, but when he drove up in a red Corvette, she laughed. "Of course," she said to herself. "Of course he has a red Corvette. What else would he have?" She tried to picture him with her own old blue car or with Adam's gray pickup, but it was an impossible picture. Anyway, it was pleasant to go out, just the two of them, to eat pizza together and walk the pier. Monday there was a band concert at the Visitors' Center. Tuesday they flew kites above the beach. Wednesday they swam at one of Wellfleet's kettle ponds. Thursday they took sandwiches to Sunset Point. Friday they went to P'town. Saturday they borrowed bicycles to ride the bike trail at Cape Race. Always they talked.

They talked of teaching and of learning, of what they liked and didn't like. He teased her about being out of condition and pushed her to use muscles she hadn't used in a long time. She tried to keep up, worrying that he would lose patience with her. She needn't have worried; his patience seemed endless. He called her Puffie and Snuffie and Guffie until she gave up trying to teach him her name and laughed, saying it didn't matter what he called her as long as he didn't forget who she was.

He had grown serious then, out on Sunset Point in the orange-red light of the giant setting sun. He had turned to look deep into her green eyes, tracing her chin with a careful touch of his fingers. "I know who you are," he said. "You're my angel. You keep me from being what I don't want to be. As long as you're with me, I know everything will be all right."

"No, Charlie, I'm not an angel. I'm just a person who cares about you. I can't make everything all right for you. I'm not powerful enough for that. I can't even do that for myself."

He had said, "Yes, you can. You're different from all the others. You're stronger, cleaner, braver. You know what you think is right and you live by it."

"I try, Charlie; I really try, but that doesn't make me an angel. It just makes me serious and dull."

He shook his head slightly, shushing her words with one finger against her lips. "You're not dull, Angel. You are definitely not dull." He brushed her lips lightly with the finger. She sat mesmerized, seeing his eyes focus on her lips, his head close and closer. His lips touched hers, very softly. She sat still, watching, barely breathing. He pulled away to study her, then bent close again for a second kiss, a firmer kiss, and she shut her eyes to close out the rest of the world.

He straightened and cleared his throat. "Sorry," he said. "I shouldn't have—"

Then she in turn silenced him with her slender finger on his lips and smiled, turning back to the sunset.

That was Thursday. On Saturday they argued. The crowd was having a party and he wanted to go. She didn't.

He went.

She didn't.

Bree argued and fussed, but Muffie held firm. She did not want to go and she was not going. She didn't want Charlie to go either. It wasn't good for him, she knew. She watched him from the apartment window as he appeared with Jack to pick up Bree. He had no girl with him, but she knew he wouldn't stay alone.

"You're making a mistake," said Bree.

"I think you are too," said Muffie. "You're going out to drink until you don't have to face the fact that you're not happy."

"Right," said Bree. "I'm going to have a good time if it kills me."

"I can't do that and I can't watch you do that either," said Muffie. "It's not for me."

Then Bree was gone, and Jack's car roared away. Muffie sat in the quiet room. She could use the time, she reasoned. She could wash her hair, rinse out a few things, straighten the mess. She was glad, really, or so she tried to convince herself, to be staying home after such a busy week. She sighed and began to pick up Bree's clothes.

When they came home she was in bed, but not asleep. From where she lay she could easily have seen the car from the window, could have looked to see if Anita sat in the back seat. She didn't look, didn't intend to let them know she was awake. On the stairs too many feet rumbled, and she could hear Jack fumbling with the key. She rose, grabbed a robe, and went to take a clumsy Bree from his care.

"Again?" she said.

Jack nodded.

"But you're sober," Muffie said. "Why do you let her do this?"

"I love her," he said.

"This is not loving her," she said. "If you love her, you can't allow this to happen. Let me put her to bed and we'll talk. Wait for me."

She was struggling with Bree's shoes when she heard the car leave. Evidently Jack didn't want to talk. She sighed. There must be something she could do, but she didn't know what it was.

It was a restless night. Between her worry about Bree

and that stupid loud bird, she got very little sleep. At five she quit trying, rose, dressed, and went out. She walked aimlessly, her steps taking her toward the harbor. She hadn't been there for a while, not alone, not since she had prayed to know what she wanted.

She still didn't have an answer, but then, she hadn't been doing a lot of listening. Adam had said she had to keep her heart open for the answer. Well, her heart had been busy lately. She'd had a lot to think about. Charlie, for one thing. It had been a wonderful week, a dream week, right down to the end, and then it had collapsed. His angel, he had called her, and the kiss had been real. But Charlie wanted what Charlie wanted, and she didn't fit the party plans.

He's stubborn, she thought, *and so am I. But at least he knows what he wants. I only know what I don't want. I don't want to go to those parties. I don't want Charlie to drink. I don't want Bree to mess up her life. I want. . .*

I want times like last week, with Charlie kind and fun. I want to help him, and help Bree. I want Bree and Jack to be happy, really happy.

She smiled. She had answers. She didn't know when she had gotten them, but she knew she had—not the whole answer, but a beginning. She still didn't know what she wanted for herself, but things were much clearer than they had been a week ago. She was absolutely certain that she would have the rest of the answer if she would wait patiently and listen. When? She didn't know, but she believed she would have her answer when she needed it. Meanwhile, she had work to do. She had to try to help Bree and Jack and Charlie.

"Thank you, Lord," she said.

How good it was to be able to talk to God! She wanted

to be with others who felt this way. In the distance she could hear the church bell. She rose and started back. She had plenty of time to make it to church, even all the way over to Adam's church. She hurried.

She entered the cool, white church about twenty minutes early, in time to hear the last of choir rehearsal and watch the choir file out. Then, except for the ushers, who were just coming in, and the organist, she was alone. This was the reason she had come early, to be alone in God's house to settle her thoughts and make herself ready for worship.

It was like coming home. She'd never been here before, but it was a place she knew. From her seat near the back she followed the light from the side windows to its bright patches on the pews, breathed in the summer air from the open windows, listened to the barely audible hum of ceiling fans, admired the altar flowers—orange lilies, probably from a nearby garden, and centered on the large cross in the front of the church. In the stillness, peace descended and she eased into it, belonging here, belonging to God, praying as naturally as breathing. She had missed this.

People were filling the pews now. A few looked somewhat familiar; some nodded and smiled. Mrs. Beale recognized her and stopped to say "good morning" before going out again. Soon Mrs. Beale was back with Adam, pointing Muffie out to him. He came directly to her and sat next to her, looking very pleased.

She smiled and rose with the congregation to begin the service. They sang together, sharing the same hymnal, prayed together, listened together. It felt right and good to worship with a friend. It would be right and good to phone home today too.

Afterward there was coffee in the Fellowship Hall, and

she was warmly greeted by those she had met before and by others who came to be introduced by Adam.

"I'm glad I came," she said on the way out. "Sunday isn't Sunday without church."

He said, "I've called several times, but no one was home."

"I've been busy," she said.

"Charlie?"

She nodded. "Charlie."

"At least let me take you to dinner," he said, walking her to her car.

She declined, saying she had to hurry to work. Then she was gone.

That wasn't nice, she thought in the car. *I shouldn't have rushed off like that. I rushed off from him last time. Adam is going to think I don't want to be around him. He'll think I'm avoiding him. Am I? Maybe. With Adam it would be too easy to slip back into Empton ways. I don't want to go backward, especially not now. I feel like my life is almost making sense. Almost. If I can just straighten a few things out. Things are so complicated with Charlie that I can't think straight.*

As usual after one of their parties, the crew at work welcomed her and she carried more than her share of the work. She didn't mind. It was a good day. When she left work to find Charlie waiting for her in the parking lot, it was an even better day.

"Hi, Angel."

"How was the party?"

"Okay. It would have been better if you had been there. I'm not used to going to parties alone."

"Alone? Where was Anita?"

"There, but not with me. You were with me, all evening.

Because of you I didn't touch a drop, not a drop. Did you know there is a whole little group at those parties that never take a drink?"

"Including Jack," she said.

"Yeah. I think he stays sober just to watch out for Bree. She drank too much."

"She often does," said Muffie. "You just never noticed before. Now she looks different to you."

"The whole party looked different," he said. "Everything looked different. I understand now what you meant about it not being for you. You knew it was wrong for you, and you stayed away even though I. . .I wish I had your strength."

"You can get strength the same place I get it. From God. Without Him I wouldn't be half this strong," she said.

"No thanks," said Charlie. "None of that religious stuff for me. I just need my angel."

She laughed. "Angels are very much involved with religious stuff."

"Do angels eat pizza?" he asked.

"This one does," she said.

And so the next week began, as the last one had, with Charlie and Muffie together most of the time. It was fun. *This is what I came for*, she thought. *I'll have to tell Adam about this when I see him.*

She didn't see Adam. She was never home to see him. On Thursday, her day off, she thought of surprising him in P'town with a picnic lunch, but it seemed foolish when she reconsidered. He wouldn't be expecting her. He probably had other plans. He might even have another girl watching the whales with him.

Bree had told her girls were always interested in the professor, but it had never occurred to Muffie before that he might be interested in them. What an idea! What an unpleasant, unwelcome, uncomfortable idea!

"Don't be childish," she scolded herself aloud. "He has every right to do as he pleases. I certainly don't mind. Not a bit. After all, I'm busy with Charlie, and he is the stuff dreams are made of."

She decided not to surprise Adam. Instead, she shopped for groceries and did her laundry. *Even party girls have housekeeping chores,* she told herself, although Bree seemed to have very few. Bree rushed from one activity to another with a desperation that left little energy for ordinary chores. In all the time that Jack and Bree spent with Charlie and Muffie, Muffie never saw Bree truly at ease. *What drives her at this frantic pace*? Muffie wondered.

She watched closely that night, with Bree's desperation in mind, and saw that she was right. Bree was in almost constant motion, chattering nonstop, turning about in the front seat to laugh and wrinkle her perfect little nose at Charlie, pointing a polished fingernail at interesting things for Charlie and Muffie to see. Through it all Jack remained steady and calm, though watchful. Now and then Muffie met Jack's glance and knew that he and she shared those thoughts about Bree. Once Muffie tried to engage Jack in conversation apart from Bree, hoping that Jack could give her some hint about Bree's behavior, but Jack neatly avoided Muffie.

To Charlie, Muffie said, "Bree seems anxious to have a good time."

"That's just the way she is," said Charlie, dismissing the subject. "Are you coming to the party Saturday? I know you don't care for parties, but this one is at the director's house and I practically have to go. I wish you'd go with me."

"It's a command performance for me too, I guess. Sure, I'd love to go with you, Charlie."

At the bottom of her stairs, he kissed her gently but firmly, ruffled her hair, watched as she climbed to the door, and left her to fumble with the key. As she pushed open the door, she heard a small thump and felt something move by her foot. A package. She took it in to the light to see what it was. She opened it to find a beautifully illustrated book, *The Audubon Society Field Guide to North American Birds,* and a tape marked "Songs of North American Small Birds." The notecard tucked inside the front cover of the book said:

> *To help you find your own song.*
> *Adam*

Adam. He had not forgotten her, had thought of her on the very day she had thought of surprising him. She took the book to the table and opened it carefully, turning pages to look at one bird after another, reading about them. Page 549-550 was turned down: "Mockingbird."

She read carefully. The mockingbird did have his own song, after all, but it was mixed in a tangle of imitations of other birds. Interesting. He hadn't lost his own song. He had only confused it with the songs of all those other birds.

Maybe she hadn't lost her own song either. It must be still with her. All she had to do was find it, listen for it.

"Listen with an open heart," she said, remembering what Adam had told her.

That night the mockingbird sang long and loudly, but

his song didn't annoy Muffie. She was busy listening to find the mockingbird's own song.

Friday was busy, as usual, and Saturday was busier. The group for her shipwreck talk was the largest yet, and the time sped. When she finished, she looked up to find Adam waiting and realized she had expected him to be there.

"Thank you for the book," she said. "I was hoping you'd come by so I could tell you how much I appreciate it. I have to go out tonight—party at the director's house—but there's time for a walk on the beach if you like."

He liked the idea, so they strolled barefoot on the hard, wet sand at the edge of the surf. They talked of whales and waves and work, and the time passed quickly. Back at the starting place, where they had left her knapsack and their shoes, they brushed the sand from their feet and put their shoes back on.

"I have to go," she said. "The party starts at seven."

He said nothing at all, but picked up her knapsack to carry it to her car. They started their separate cars, waved lightly, and drove toward the main road. Looking back at his car, she saw him watching her and waved again, hoping he remembered to look where he was driving. "Stop sign," she said, as if he could hear her. He stopped. She turned right and he turned left. She watched his car disappear in the traffic.

She took care with her looks that night. She didn't know the director well, but she liked what she knew and wanted to make a good impression. At least she knew how to dress for this kind of party. Her white silky pants (not real silk, of course) and sea-green blouse, the color that brought out the green in her eyes, were just right. She knew she looked neat and clean and, according to the mirror, rather pretty.

Bree looked perfect, as usual, also in white silk (real silk) pants and royal blue silk shirt. This was a conservative look for her, but in some ways it suited her better. In these clothes Bree seemed elegant but fragile—lovely. She was slow getting ready though, moving as if half asleep.

"What's the matter, Bree?" Muffie asked. "Are you all right?"

"Sure. I'm fine."

Only three words? Muffie thought that was odd all by itself. She watched Bree move clumsily across the room to find her sandals. She moved almost like she did when she had been drinking.

"Have you been drinking?" Muffie asked.

"Just a couple of drinks. Getting a headstart on the party. Director doesn't serve alcohol, so I have to bring my own."

A car pulled up in front and they heard Charlie call, "Angel?"

"Angel!" Bree exclaimed. "He calls you Angel. What have you done to Charlie?"

"Nothing," said Muffie.

"He's crazy about you," said Bree. "Charlie Cooper is so crazy about you he doesn't even see all the girls trying to get his attention. I don't know how you did it, but nobody else ever did."

"That's what you wanted, isn't it?" Muffie asked.

"Yeah, but I didn't expect it to go this far. And I expected that you'd be crazy about him too."

"I am," said Muffie. "He's terrific fun."

"And handsome and intelligent and kind, and you don't sound like a girl who's crazy about him. What's the matter with you? Charlie's a one-in-a-million man and you treat him like he's an ordinary guy. He's not. He's wonderful."

"Like Jack?"

"No," said Bree. "Like nobody else. There's only one Charlie and if I had your chance, I'd jump at it."

Muffie said, "You have a chance—Jack, only you won't accept his love."

"Jack isn't Charlie," said Bree. "I like Jack, but Charlie I lo—" Bree broke off suddenly, hand over her mouth, eyes wide.

"Love," finished Muffie, softly, knowing as she said it that this was true. "You love Charlie. That's the whole trouble, isn't it? That's why you never say yes to Jack." Muffie thought a moment, then added, "But if you love Charlie, why did you try to fasten him to me?"

"It was a mistake," Bree said bitterly. "I thought he'd get tired of you and see me waiting right there under his nose. I thought if we four spent enough time together he'd remember what fun he used to have with me. I thought you were too dull for him. I was wrong. He thinks you're his angel."

"I'm sorry," said Muffie. "I didn't know."

"Neither does Jack. And Charlie can't see anybody but you."

"And you're miserable."

"Yes," said Bree, "I'm miserable. I tried to hate you, but I can't. I try to be in love with Jack, but I'm not. I try to forget Charlie, but I can't."

"So you drink."

Bree nodded, tears in her eyes.

"It won't help, Bree."

"I know."

"You have to stop. You're too important to do this to yourself, Bree. You're important to Jack and to me. We care what happens to you."

"Charlie doesn't," she sobbed. "Charlie doesn't even notice."

Muffie held her while she cried, then Bree dried her tears, blew her nose, washed her face. They both exchanged their wet blouses for fresh dark blue blouses.

"I wish I could hate you," said Bree, sniffling.

"I'm glad you don't," said Muffie. "Just let me help you."

Bree nodded and came quietly down the stairs with Muffie to the car. Jack took one close look at Bree and turned a questioning glance at Muffie, who shook her head to indicate that it was better to pretend not to notice the reddened eyes and sniffly nose. Charlie helped Muffie into the back seat and they were off.

This party was better, in Muffie's opinion. It was quieter, more civilized. Subtle music filled the empty corners of the background; the buffet was a feast of beautifully prepared delicacies; the evening air on the huge deck overlooking the sea was balmy. It was a lovely party. Muffie lost sight of Jack and Bree and began to relax. Charlie moved with her from group to group, doing what he was so good at, mixing with people of all kinds. Somehow they got separated, but that was all right. Her mother had taught her that the way to be a good guest was to try to talk a little bit with each guest, as well as with the hosts, so she began to search for those she had not yet spoken with.

That was when she noticed Adam. He was standing in the corner of the deck with two people who were carrying on a conversation that should have involved him, but he was not really involved. He was standing absolutely still, watching her. Their eyes met and he smiled a very small, private smile. She smiled back and moved toward him.

"You didn't say you were coming," she said.

He said, "The director is an old friend of mine. You look beautiful tonight."

"So do you," she said, seeing the way his blue blazer made his deep blue eyes even bluer. "I've never seen you so dressed up before. I almost don't recognize you."

"It's just me," he said. "Me and my brand new jacket. I was hoping to impress you."

"I'm impressed. I'm seriously impressed. It still has all its buttons and not one wrinkle. You must be—"

Glass shattered somewhere across the room, and Bree's laugh rang out in the abrupt silence. Muffie started immediately toward Bree, saying a hurried "excuse me" and easing through the crowd.

Jack was there before her. "I'll take her home," he said.

"I'll come too," said Muffie. "You might need me. I'll tell Charlie."

In no time they had made a quick, not too graceful exit and deposited Bree in the front seat.

"What happened?" asked Muffie, as they drove off.

"Put her glass down on a table that wasn't there. She acts like she's had too much to drink," said Jack. "Brought it with her, I think. I don't know. I've never seen her like this."

"It's not just the drinking," said Muffie. "She was upset before we came. If we get her home, maybe I can get her quieted down."

Bree was not quiet now. She laughed and shouted and bounced, while the other three tried to calm her.

Charlie said, "Maybe I can hold her in her seat if you

put her back here with us."

Bree unfastened her seat belt and turned to him. "Yes, let Charlie hold me. I want Charlie to hold me." She lurched to her feet to reach to him.

"Look out," shouted Charlie, springing up to catch her. He missed.

Bree wavered, screamed, and was gone.

Jack slammed on the brakes and swerved, throwing Charlie out onto the pavement. Muffie screamed, the car screeched to a stop, and all was still.

Jack was out first, bending over Bree, who lay crumpled and broken in the gravel at the side of the road. Charlie was closer to the car and in the road. Muffie ran to him. He was breathing, but unconscious. He didn't move. "Help us, Lord," she prayed, not caring who heard as long as God was listening.

A car was coming. Visible in the night because of her white pants, she waved it down. The car had a CB and in a very few minutes the police and the rescue squad arrived. They took Bree and Charlie.

"Go with them, Jack," she said. "I'll bring your car."

The rescue team vanished in the flash of lights, and she followed the police car more slowly. The hospital was far, very far, or it seemed far. It seemed to take years to get there. She arrived numb and frightened. One of the policemen led her to the emergency room, where she found Jack. She hugged him and held him, but she knew he didn't feel it.

The policeman wanted a statement. She answered his questions as well as she could, trying to remember details, losing them in the confusion. Jack was being questioned on the other side of the room. He submitted to the breath test the police requested when they learned the hospital had found alcohol in Bree's blood.

One of the police officers asked if she wanted him to call someone. Muffie couldn't think. There was no one. She couldn't—*Adam. He would know what to do. He was probably still at the party.*

"Call Adam," she said, searching her purse for the phone number.

nine

Minutes passed, stretched long by anxiety. Jack paced and sat and paced again. Muffie sat on the edge of a chair, alert to the comings and goings of the professional staff. Surely someone would come soon to tell them Bree and Charlie were all right. What was taking so long?

Adam came at last, but Muffie remained tightly tuned to the people around her. Adam spoke quietly to the staff and returned to say there was no news yet, but that they would hear as soon as the doctors knew anything.

Almost on his heels came a doctor. Muffie tensed and moved to Jack's side.

The doctor spoke in even, quiet tones, "The young man is suffering some broken bones and some severe bruises. He's in the operating room right now. He should be all right, but he's going to need some care."

Muffie felt weak with relief. Charlie was going to be all right.

The doctor continued, "I'm afraid the young lady is gone. There was nothing we could do. She seems to have struck her head in the fall, and there was only the slimmest chance she could live. I'm sorry."

"She's *dead*?" came the strangled cry from Jack.

"I'm sorry," said the doctor.

Bree! Perfect Bree! thought Muffie. *She can't be dead. She can't be!* She heard sobbing and remembered Jack, turning to him in shock and grief. They sat together, huddling in misery on the green plastic sofa.

"I'll take you home," said Adam at last.

Muffie shook her head. "I'll wait for Charlie," she said and settled down to wait next to Jack, who sat where he was, too stricken to respond.

Adam nodded and went to bring coffee and then to call a friend to take Jack in for the night, rather than leave Jack alone in his house. For Muffie there was no family nearby. Adam's instinct was to keep her with him, watching over her until he was sure she would be all right, but on careful thought he decided to call Mrs. Beale. Muffie would be safe at her house.

At the same time Muffie began going over and over her failure to help Bree. If only she had done more. If only she had warned Jack of Bree's dangerous mood, or done more to slow down Bree's drinking. If only she had stayed closer to Bree at the party, if only. . .

"You couldn't have known this would happen," said Adam.

"I have to—there must be something I can do. Let me think," said Muffie. She searched for something, something to make it all better. "Someone should call Bree's mother," she said.

Perhaps the phone number would be in Bree's belongings. Adam asked the nurse for them and found a home address.

"I'll call," Adam said.

"I'll do it," Muffie said. "I have to do it."

The operator found the number and Muffie woke Bree's mother to say the words that would bring her such terrible pain. Struggling for words of comfort, she left her number with Bree's mother, saying she would call again tomorrow to see what she could do to help.

She should call Charlie's family, she supposed, but that could wait until morning, until he could tell them himself.

What else? Notify the Visitors' Center in the morning. Get Jack's car back to him. She groped for other details to make right. "Adam, what should I do?"

"Wait. Pray. It's all you can do. For now it's enough."

It was a long time. They kept their vigil into the small hours of the morning. Somewhere in that time Adam took her hands. Sometime he put his arm around her and pulled her close. She was unaware of these things when they happened, but his strength comforted her. From time to time she spoke, not always coherently. He listened to her go over the accident again and again. He watched her pale face for signs of tears, but there were none. She carried on an irregular conversation with God, a painful conversation that was part prayer, part search for understanding, part simple awareness of His presence.

Almost three hours after the accident, Charlie was wheeled out of the recovery room. The nurse said they could see him, so they followed her directions to his room.

He lay still, a mound of white bandages on a white bed. Muffie came to stand near him, taking the fingers of one bandaged hand in her hand.

"Angel?" he whispered.

"Here, Charlie."

"Angel, Bree—"

"She's dead, Charlie."

"I couldn't. . .she. . ."

"I know, Charlie. It's not your fault."

Charlie struggled to sit up and barely moved. "Jack?"

"Here," said Jack.

"I'm sorry, Jack. I'm—" Charlie whispered, ending in a choked sob.

Still holding Charlie's fingers, Muffie murmured. "It's not your fault, Charlie. It's not your fault. Sleep. Go to sleep." She brushed the loose hair from his temples and stroked his cheek. His breathing gradually steadied and quieted. He slept.

She released his fingers and leaned to kiss him gently on the forehead.

Adam said, "The nurse says he'll sleep until late morning. We need to get Jack home. He's exhausted. You can come back tomorrow when he's awake." He pulled her firmly to the door. With one arm on Jack's shoulders and one on Muffie's shoulders, he managed to guide them out into the night.

In the crowded pickup, Jack hunched against the door in silent grief. He was aware of the things around him, but they didn't matter. Muffie sat in silence too, staring blankly at the road. She began to shiver, lightly at first, then violently. Adam stopped the car to wrap her in his new jacket, heedless of wrinkles. He held her close, murmuring to her. He didn't know what the words were or even if they were real words, but they didn't matter. They soothed her so that she grew calmer.

He began to drive again, trying to keep one hand free to hold her next to him. She took no notice of his driving, but it was all right. He was concentrating, taking no chances with this precious cargo.

They delivered Jack to his friend's home, where the friend led him inside. Then Adam drove Muffie to Mrs. Beale's home, coming to a gentle stop in front of the small white cottage. He turned to hold her in his arms as the first of her tears came and then grew to great gulping sobs.

"I should have stopped her," she sobbed. "I didn't try hard enough. I should have been—"

"Hush," he said.

"I have to call the Center," she sobbed, "and get Jack's car, and—"

"Hush," he said.

"I have to—"

"No, you don't. You don't have to do anything at all. Hush."

"But I have to take care of—"

"You don't always have to be the one who takes care of things."

"Yes, I do," she wept. "I always do. That's who I am. I'm not a Muffie. I'm a M . . . Mar . . . Martha," and she sobbed harder.

In spite of himself, Adam chuckled. "I'm so glad you're a Martha," he whispered, "but even a Martha can't take care of everything. Hush, Martha, hush."

Eventually the sobs subsided and he eased her out of the car and into the arms of Mrs. Beale. "I'll take care of her," Mrs. Beale promised.

"She needs—"

"I know," said Mrs. Beale. "I'll take good care of your Muffie."

"Martha," he said, tasting the new name and finding it good. "Her name is Martha."

She should have slept all day, according to Mrs. Beale, but Martha was up by nine, wakened by the smell of breakfast and the distant peal of a bell. A church bell—and she knew immediately she must go to church. She had only the clothes she'd come in and they were crushed. No, Mrs. Beale had run them through the washer and dryer and they were fresh and clean. She showered and dressed, distantly aware of the pleasure of being in a real house with plumbing that worked and rooms that were neat and uncluttered. That was a big improvement over the mess Bree always—

Bree.

After church she must phone Bree's mother again to see what she could do to help. And she must talk to Charlie's father to make sure he understood how Charlie had tried to save Bree. It was important that Charlie's father know that, and she knew Charlie wouldn't say it. She had to see Charlie today, had to be there when he was awake, had to help him. And Jack would need someone too. There was so much to do, *". . .but even a Martha can't take care of everything."*

Adam had said that last night. This morning.

She needed to see him, to thank him for being there. And she still had his jacket.

Adam was already in church when she and Mrs. Beale arrived. They joined him in his pew halfway down the center aisle. *This must be his regular seat*, thought Martha; *Mrs. Beale knew just where to find him.*

He looked a little tired, but not bad. He looked better than she felt she looked. Her eyes still burned from crying, and she knew they were puffy. Charlie should like that; he had called her Puffie once and now it fit.

She was weary, too weary to take in all the details of the service or to follow the sermon as carefully as she should have, but the feeling of worship restored her, rested her in ways the short sleep had not. How foolish she had been to avoid church! For that matter, how foolish she had been to try to change herself into a good-time girl. She was what she was—a Martha. She sighed.

Adam turned at the sound of her sigh, lifting his brows in question. She smiled slightly to let him know it was all right and tried to concentrate on the sermon.

She had to call Bree's mother. She wanted to call her own mother and father too.

She tried to concentrate on the sermon. Then they were singing and closing with prayer.

"I'm glad I came," she whispered in the general subdued murmur of after-church exodus.

Adam smiled, "You said that last time."

"It's always true," she said.

She was anxious to get to Charlie, she explained to Mrs. Beale, so she would have to miss the coffee hour this time. She hugged Mrs. Beale and thanked her, but Mrs. Beale wouldn't accept so quick a dismissal of her aid. She insisted that Martha stay with her another night and refused to think otherwise. Martha was grateful to accept. Going back to an apartment devoid of Bree's chatter would be hard enough in daylight. Night alone there would be difficult.

Jack and his friend would pick up his car today, Adam said, so all they had to do was call the Center, which Martha did from the church office. She told them only that Bree and Charlie would not be in, and that she'd be a little late. She would explain later.

She also called Bree's mother and offered to send Bree's things home.

They picked up a sandwich and a Coke at a fast food place and ate in Adam's car. It was a good enough lunch. She didn't taste it anyway. It didn't occur to her to wonder why he was driving her down there. He just seemed to assume he would, and she accepted that.

Charlie was awake but a little hazy. He remembered little of the night, but the accident itself was clear and immediate in his mind. He wanted to talk about it, so they did, several times over. He couldn't get past the part where he reached for Bree and missed her. He seemed to feel that if he had been quicker or stronger or something, she wouldn't have fallen. They reassured him, but they knew it would take a while for him to learn to live with the memory.

He hadn't called his father, so Martha called and held the phone for him to talk. Then she talked, explaining that Charlie had been wonderful, that he was hurt because he had tried to save Bree at great risk to himself, and that Charlie's family should be proud of him. It was quiet on the other end of the line as Mr. Cooper absorbed all this. He asked to speak to Charlie again, so she held the phone for him while Charlie nodded and said "Uh huh," and "Good-bye," and finally smiled. She hung up.

"Thanks, Angel," he said. "He's coming here. He says he's proud of me. He wouldn't have said that if you hadn't talked to him." To Adam he said, "That's why I call her Angel. She makes things come out right for me."

Martha said, "I'm not an angel, Charlie."

He said, "You are to me. Besides, I can't call you Muffie. It doesn't fit you."

"Call me by my name then, Charlie," she said. "I'm Martha."

"Martha? Really?" He sounded doubtful. "I don't know about 'Martha.' I like 'Angel' better. Either one is better than Muffie. What did you want to be called that for?"

"It sounded fun," she said, feeling foolish.

Charlie said, "You've seen one Muffie, you've seen 'em all."

She laughed. "You always say that, Charlie, and you know you don't believe it."

"I know," he laughed. "It's a habit left over from college. I guess I've outgrown it. It's time I outgrew a lot of things. I haven't grown enough; I only got bigger."

"You're going to be all right, Charlie," Martha said. "You're going to be terrific. Got to go to work, but I'll be back." She kissed him lightly on the forehead.

Charlie said, "I'll wait here for you, Angel."

Driving back in the Sunday afternoon beach traffic was slow, but Adam drove carefully, refusing to rush. She was a little late for work, as she expected, but no one objected, especially when she sought out her shift manager and explained about Bree and Charlie. The shift manager seemed to be impressed that Martha was there and said she could go home if she liked, but Martha wanted to stay, wanted to be too busy to think.

The news about Bree and Charlie traveled fast, and she spent most of the afternoon answering inquiries about the accident. Saying over and over that Bree was dead didn't make it seem real to her, but she knew she would have to face it. It simply seemed impossible. She was still a little shaky, and she knew Jack would be too.

She phoned him and he responded listlessly, but with more life than he'd had when they'd brought him home.

"I loved her," he said, over and over. "I loved her."

At least Charlie will be fine, she thought. As soon as she left work she would go see him again, pick up clean clothes at home, and go back to Mrs. Beale's.

That's exactly what she did, except that Adam was there

to meet her after work and drive her to Charlie. Adam didn't have much to say during the visit, not as much as he had to say at their earlier visit. He sat in a far corner of the room and watched. She didn't notice; Adam was often quiet.

She was very tired when they left the hospital. To Adam's suggestion that they stop for supper, she said she'd rather not; she wasn't hungry. He was hungry, he said, so if she didn't mind watching him, he'd like to eat something. They stopped at a modest-looking family restaurant and she ordered iced tea. He got the whole meatloaf dinner, complete with fruit cup, salad, rolls, fries, and green beans.

"Want a bite?" he said, holding out the fruit cup and the spoon.

She ate a bite. Then she ate the whole fruit cup. He asked for an extra fork so she could have some salad, and she did. Then she ate the rolls, half the meatloaf, and most of the fries.

"It's a good thing you weren't hungry," he said.

She blinked and looked embarrassed. He laughed and ordered two strawberry shortcakes, then watched her methodically eat her way through the large dessert.

"I feel better," she said.

"You will tomorrow, when you've had some sleep. Let's get you home."

At Mrs. Beale's front door she said, "Thank you for taking care of me. I'm not used to it."

"You must have someone at home that you go out with. He must take care of you," he said.

"I don't think I ever let him take care of me," she said. "I was too busy taking care of everything else."

"In that case," he said, "he wasn't the right person for you."

"No," she said.

She wanted to think this strange conversation through that night, tried to stay awake to reason out what it meant, but she was too tired. She slipped into deep sleep almost as soon as she laid her head on the pillow.

In the morning she returned to the apartment to pack Bree's things, using all those boxes from the grocery that she had used to make temporary shelves. She folded each lovely item carefully, feeling that this was something, a last something, she could do for Bree. As she packed, she thought of the sparkling, lively girl who had loved Charlie and wondered if Charlie knew how much Bree had loved him. Martha would never tell him. If he didn't know, perhaps it was better he didn't. It certainly would be better for Jack not to know.

She found a few pictures of Bree and kept one for herself and one for Jack. She also found a small box of keepsakes from special times—a seashell, a button, a program from a concert, and other things of little value except for memory. Perhaps Jack would want these.

She called him and he came over. He was still distant and a little vague, but he was making an effort. Yes, he wanted the picture. The box of keepsakes? He opened it and thoughtfully handled each item, putting each back in the box and closing the lid.

"These aren't mine," he said quietly. "These must be Charlie's. She loved him. I knew it, but I thought maybe, if I waited and loved her long enough, she'd get around to loving me back. She never did."

Martha said, "She must have loved you in her own way. She just didn't know it yet. Maybe, if there'd been more time—"

"Yes," he said. "Maybe." He handed her the box. "Thanks."

He helped her seal the boxes and send them. That was all there was to do.

"Thanks," he said again.

"Visit Charlie," she said, "for your own sake as well as his."

He nodded.

She worked, ate, visited Charlie with Adam, phoned home, slept. Tuesday was much the same. Wednesday she got the day off to drive with Adam and Jack to a small New Hampshire town for Bree's funeral. They stood together in the cemetery, saying good-bye to Bree, then went back to her mother's house for coffee and cake before returning late at night to Cape Cod. It was all so fast.

Charlie was restless and moody. He was discontent, eager to be on his feet. She could understand that. He must also have been lonely, although that seemed impossible considering all the company he had. Someone had brought a guest book and the signatures went on and on. His room was filled with cards and flowers. Nurses came and went constantly, glad to do whatever they could think of to spend time with this handsome, charming man. He had music in the room and newspapers. The phone rang all day.

His family spent time with him, pleasantly supportive and encouraging. She had met the formidable father and had words with him about Charlie. His father seemed taken aback by her forthright statements, but he listened and came to a different, broader appreciation of his son's success.

Charlie seemed to have everything, but he was not satisfied.

She asked him about it the next Sunday. "What's wrong,

Charlie? What can I do for you?"

"What is it you have that gives you the power to make your life worth living?" he said. "I lie here and think about how empty my life is. Then I see you and see how you live and wonder what makes you like you are. You're a tough lady. You stood right up to me and right up to my father. I think you could stand up to anybody. Adam has this strength too."

"I told you, Charlie," Martha said. "That strength comes from the Lord. When you belong to Him, you become different. You think different things; you want different things. Your values change. Some things you just don't do because you know He doesn't want you to."

"Like drink," Charlie said.

"Like drink," she agreed. "The Bible says that we should not be drunk, and so we avoid it."

"The Bible actually says that?" asked Charlie.

From his corner Adam said, "It's in Ephesians, chapter five, I think." He pulled a small Testament from his pocket and flipped pages. "Here it is. Ephesians 5: 18. 'And be not drunk with wine, wherein is excess; but be filled with the Spirit.'"

"I want this strength," Charlie said. "I want strength like yours."

"Are you sure?" Martha asked. "If you turn your life over to God, you don't know where you'll end up. You might find yourself going to church."

"I can do that," Charlie said.

"Then all you have to do is pray to God and ask Him to come into your heart. Adam and I will pray with you, but you have to do your own asking. I can't do that for you."

Charlie nodded. The three joined hands in the hospital

room and prayed, and Charlie opened his heart to God. Afterward they hugged and smiled and laughed.

Martha was still smiling in the car. "I don't know when I've felt so good about anything," she said. "Charlie is special; he's wonderful. I've been so worried about him, and now I know he's going to be all right."

"Yes," said Adam. He hesitated, then he said, "Do you know the rest of that chapter in Ephesians?"

"No," she said. "I must have heard it and read it, but I don't remember it. Why?"

He handed her the Testament. "Find it," he said. "Ephesians five."

She found it.

"Read it," he said.

She read, "'And be not drunk with wine, wherein is excess; but be filled with the Spirit. . .'"

"Go on."

"'Speaking to yourselves in psalms and hymns and spiritual songs, singing and making melody in your heart to the Lord'. . .I like that," she said. "It's like having your own song to sing in your heart."

"Exactly," he said. "Your own song, not somebody else's."

"My song."

"Yes."

"My song for the Lord."

"Yes."

She lay awake that night, listening to the mockingbird, trying to find his own song in the tangle of measures borrowed from other birds. *Poor bird*, she thought, and was glad she had her own song. She had her own self too, such as it was. She was Martha—serious, responsible Martha—

but she sang in her heart. And she had learned a few things. She knew how to have fun, thanks to Charlie. Thanks to Adam, she knew how to accept kindness and caring.

This wasn't what she had prayed for. She had prayed to know what she wanted, and she didn't exactly know yet. Not all of it, anyway. She had wanted Charlie to be happy, and she felt certain he was on the way to that happiness. She had wanted to help Bree and Jack, but she hadn't been able to do that. She would probably always wish she had done more, but it was too late for Bree. Muffie had wanted to be a party girl and she wasn't, but she did know how to have fun. She had wanted a summer to remember. She had that. She had wanted to be different; she wasn't entirely different, but there were changes. At least she knew who she was. She knew now that she could learn to be content to be herself.

Martha visited Charlie every day. Occasionally Martha visited without Adam, but usually he drove her there and sat quietly in his corner listening to them talk, hold hands, laugh. Each time they left, Adam stood to shake hands and watched as she kissed Charlie lightly on the forehead or cheek in good-bye.

Charlie seemed to improve almost as they watched. He sat up. They pushed him in a wheelchair. He stood. He walked a little. Then one evening he told them he was to be released in a day or so. For the rest of the summer he would be useless as a lifeguard and really couldn't work at much else for a while, but he should be able to start teaching on time when school started. His father wanted him to come home until he could take better care of himself.

"Wonderful," said Martha.

"But I don't want to go," Charlie said. "I can't go. I

can't lose you. I've finally found my own angel and I want to keep her. I need you, Angel."

"No, you don't. You just think you do. You'll see."

He reached for her and pulled her close, kissing her firmly on the lips. "Marry me, Angel."

Marry Charlie! Beautiful Charlie wanted to marry her.

"Angel?"

"But Charlie. . ."

But Charlie, I'm Martha, dull, reliable Martha, she thought. *How can you want to marry me?*

"I need you, Angel. Marry me."

"I—yes. Yes, Charlie."

Neither of them noticed Adam leave as Charlie kissed her again.

Charlie said, "We'll be a great team, you and me. We'll raise a family, take them to Sunday school, love them to pieces. I'll coach and make you proud of me."

"I'm already proud of you, Charlie."

"Yeah, I know. You make me better than I am. You make me worth something." Charlie spun the future before her, and it floated there like a shining ribbon, like a rainbow dragon in the sky.

He needed her. She had always wanted to be useful and here it was, a future of being important to him and useful. Listening to his plans she pictured it all, growing old with him, laughing.

"Angel?"

"Yes?"

"What do you think?"

"About what?"

"Weren't you listening? I was telling you about the house I want to build for us."

"Yes, Charlie. I guess I'm still getting used to the idea."

He talked on and on and she listened, or she thought she was listening. Evidently she wasn't, for she came to attention to find him silent, watching her. Had he asked her something she hadn't heard? She tried to remember.

"I'm sorry," she said. "I must have—" She stopped, confused.

"Look at me, Angel," he said. "Do you want to marry me?"

She thought. *Any girl in her right mind would want to marry Charlie. Of course I want to marry Charlie.* She said, "Don't be silly, Charlie. Any girl in her right mind would—"

"Not *any* girl," he said. "*You.* Do you want to marry me?"

She hesitated. "No," she said, her voice so low he couldn't hear it. She cleared her throat. "No," she said a little louder, her own voice sounding foreign in her ears. But it was true. It was crazy, but it was true. She didn't want to marry Charlie. "I'm sorry," she said.

He studied her in her confusion. She was lovely—an angel, but not his angel. He held her hand in his, stroking the long, strong fingers. He hadn't anticipated this and neither had she. She was struggling to regain her composure, but she was losing the struggle. He needed her, he wanted her, but what did she need? What did she want? He wished he knew so he could give it to her. She had given him so much.

Adam might know, he thought. Adam seemed to know her better than anyone else. He was always with her, always in the background, watching over her.

Adam, he thought. He said it aloud, "Adam."

She looked at him blankly. "Adam," she said. She turned to him in his corner, but he was gone. "Adam? Oh, Charlie, I—"

"I know, Angel."

She shrugged helplessly.

"Good-bye, Angel," Charlie said, but she was already gone.

Adam wasn't in the hall. She moved more rapidly to the elevator, pushing the down button, impatient for it to open its doors, impatient for it to close its doors. She willed it to hurry. On the main floor she looked quickly around. Not there. She sped to the door and then to the dark parking lot and his car.

She saw him then, in a circle of light in the parking lot. He was slouched against the far side of his car, bent over, alone.

"Adam," she called. He didn't look up. She ran to him. "Adam," she said in barely suppressed excitement.

"Congratulations," he said, raising his head and forcing a smile. "I hope you'll be very happy."

"I will be, Adam," she said, "but not with Charlie."

"Not with Charlie? But you said 'yes'."

"Charlie doesn't need me, not any more. And I don't want to be an angel. I'm a real person and I want—"

"What do you want, Martha?"

"You, Adam. I want you."

He folded her in his arms, burying his face in her hair. "Are you sure?"

"I love you, Adam. And you need me. I can sew on your buttons and tell you when the light is red. I can.—"

"You can let me love you, honor you, and cherish you. I love you, Martha. I've loved you since the day we met in

Provincetown. I loved you when you tried to be a Muffie. When you said yes to Charlie I thought my heart would stop. Marry me, Martha."

"Yes, Adam," she said, from safe in his arms. "That's exactly what I want to do."

NOTE

Wellfleet and Provincetown don't need imagination to make them romantic. They are romantic enough in reality. There are boats at Provincetown for whale-watching, but the *Minke II* was created just for this book.

The National Seashore and its facilities mentioned in this book are real and at least as wonderful as I have described them to be, but the organization, management, personnel, and summer program for teachers are entirely from my imagination. Any resemblance to reality is entirely accidental.

A Letter To Our Readers

Dear Reader:

In order that we might better contribute to your reading enjoyment, we would appreciate your taking a few minutes to respond to the following questions. When completed, please return to the following:

Rebecca Germany, Editor
Heartsong Presents
P.O. Box 719
Uhrichsville, Ohio 44683

1. Did you enjoy reading *Mockingbird's Song*?
   ❏ Very much. I would like to see more books
      by this author!
   ❏ Moderately
      I would have enjoyed it more if _____

   _____

2. Are you a member of **Heartsong Presents**? ❏Yes ❏No
   If no, where did you purchase this book? _____

   _____

3. What influenced your decision to purchase this
   book? (Check those that apply.)

   ❏ Cover   ❏ Back cover copy

   ❏ Title   ❏ Friends

   ❏ Publicity   ❏ Other_____

4. How would you rate, on a scale from 1 (poor) to 5
   (superior), **Heartsong Presents'** new cover design?_____

5. On a scale from 1 (poor) to 10 (superior), please rate the following elements.

    ___Heroine   ___Plot

    ___Hero   ___Inspirational theme

    ___Setting   ___Secondary characters

6. What settings would you like to see covered in **Heartsong Presents** books?_____

_____

_____

7. What are some inspirational themes you would like to see treated in future books?_____

_____

_____

8. Would you be interested in reading other **Heartsong Presents** titles?   ❏ Yes   ❏ No

9. Please check your age range:
  ❏ Under 18   ❏ 18-24   ❏ 25-34
  ❏ 35-45   ❏ 46-55   ❏ Over 55

10. How many hours per week do you read? _____

Name _____

Occupation_____

Address _____

City_____ State_____ Zip _____

Norma Jean Lutz

__*Fields of Sweet Content*__—When Alecia is summoned to Oklahoma by her sister, she never expected to be in the classroom again, as well as, become the key to unlock the prison of sorrow surrounding a father and his daughter. HP41 $2.95.

__*Love's Silken Melody*__—Roshelle Ramone is a star, yet deep, hidden memories and feelings of guilt continue to haunt and paralyze her. Even Victor Moran, the handsome recording company owner, who truly loves her, cannot reach past the darkness of Rochelle's past. HP57 $2.95.

___*Cater to a Whim*__—God promised to bless Bandy in all her endeavors, didn't he? Just when things seem to be turning around for Bandy, they fall apart again. An underhanded employee tries to sabotage her business and the new man in Bandy's life seems to be working with her enemies. HP90 $2.95.

__*The Winning Heart*__—Kassie's life in Virginia with her sister Glorene is a stifling contrast to the wide open spaces of Kassie's former ranch existence. Through work at a stables Kassie meets Loren, a man who loves horses as much as she. But as she and Loren are drawn closer, Kassie finds herself being pulled deeper into the dark world of politics and double-dealing. HP121 $2.95.

·····Hearts♥ng·····

Any 12 *Heartsong Presents* titles for only $26.95 ★★

CONTEMPORARY ROMANCE IS CHEAPER BY THE DOZEN!

Buy any assortment of twelve *Heartsong Presents* titles and save 25% off of the already discounted price of $2.95 each!

★★plus $1.00 shipping and handling per order and sales tax where applicable.

HEARTSONG PRESENTS TITLES AVAILABLE NOW:

__HP 3 RESTORE THE JOY, *Sara Mitchell*
__HP 4 REFLECTIONS OF THE HEART, *Sally Laity**
__HP 5 THIS TREMBLING CUP, *Marlene Chase*
__HP 6 THE OTHER SIDE OF SILENCE, *Marlene Chase*
__HP 9 HEARTSTRINGS, *Irene B. Brand**
__HP 10 SONG OF LAUGHTER, *Lauraine Snelling**
__HP 13 PASSAGE OF THE HEART, *Kjersti Hoff Baez*
__HP 14 A MATTER OF CHOICE, *Susannah Hayden*
__HP 18 LLAMA LADY, *VeraLee Wiggins**
__HP 19 ESCORT HOMEWARD, *Eileen M. Berger**
__HP 21 GENTLE PERSUASION, *Veda Boyd Jones*
__HP 22 INDY GIRL, *Brenda Bancroft*
__HP 25 REBAR, *Mary Carpenter Reid*
__HP 26 MOUNTAIN HOUSE, *Mary Louise Colln*
__HP 29 FROM THE HEART, *Sara Mitchell*
__HP 30 A LOVE MEANT TO BE, *Brenda Bancroft*
__HP 33 SWEET SHELTER, *VeraLee Wiggins*
__HP 34 UNDER A TEXAS SKY, *Veda Boyd Jones*
__HP 37 DRUMS OF SHELOMOH, *Yvonne Lehman*
__HP 38 A PLACE TO CALL HOME, *Eileen M. Berger*
__HP 41 FIELDS OF SWEET CONTENT, *Norma Jean Lutz*
__HP 42 SEARCH FOR TOMORROW, *Mary Hawkins*
__HP 45 DESIGN FOR LOVE, *Janet Gortsema*
__HP 46 THE GOVERNOR'S DAUGHTER, *Veda Boyd Jones*
__HP 49 YESTERDAY'S TOMORROWS, *Linda Herring*
__HP 50 DANCE IN THE DISTANCE, *Kjersti Hoff Baez*
__HP 53 MIDNIGHT MUSIC, *Janelle Burnham*
__HP 54 HOME TO HER HEART, *Lena Nelson Dooley*
__HP 57 LOVE'S SILKEN MELODY, *Norma Jean Lutz*
__HP 58 FREE TO LOVE, *Doris English*
__HP 61 PICTURE PERFECT, *Susan Kirby*
__HP 62 A REAL AND PRECIOUS THING, *Brenda Bancroft*
__HP 65 ANGEL FACE, *Frances Carfi Matranga*
__HP 66 AUTUMN LOVE, *Ann Bell*
__HP 69 BETWEEN LOVE AND LOYALTY, *Susannah Hpyden*
__HP 70 A NEW SONG, *Kathleen Yapp*
__HP 73 MIDSUMMER'S DREAM, *Rena Eastman*
__HP 74 SANTANONI SUNRISE, *Hope Irvin Marston and Claire M. Coughlin*
__HP 77 THE ROAD BEFORE ME, *Susannah Hayden**
__HP 78 A SIGN OF LOVE, *Veda Boyd Jones**
__HP 81 BETTER THAN FRIENDS, *Sally Laity*

*Temporarily out of stock

(If ordering from this page, please remember to include it with the order form.)

Presents

*Temporarily out of stock.

Great Inspirational Romance at a Great Price!

Heartsong Presents books are inspirational romances in contemporary and historical settings, designed to give you an enjoyable, spirit-lifting reading experience. You can choose from 148 wonderfully written titles from some of today's best authors like Colleen L. Reece, Brenda Bancroft, Janelle Jamison, and many others.

When ordering quantities less than twelve, above titles are $2.95 each.